BLIND READER WANTED

(Only Females Need Apply)

Georgia Le Carre

ALSO BY GEORGIA

The Billionaire Banker Series

Owned
42 Days
Besotted
Seduce Me
Love's Sacrifice

Masquerade

Pretty Wicked (novella)

Disfigured Love

Hypnotized

Crystal Jake

Sexy Beast

Wounded Beast

Beautiful Beast

Dirty Aristocrat

You Don't Own Me 1 & 2

The Bad Boy Wants Me

You Don't Know Me

Beauty and the Dark

Click on the link below to receive news of my latest releases and exclusive content.

http://bit.ly/10e9WdE

Editors: Caryl Milton, Elizabeth Burns
Contributors: Shannon Lee & IS Creations
Cover Designer: http://www.bookcoverbydesign.co.uk
Proofreader: http:// http://nicolarheadediting.com/

The Blind Reader

Published by Georgia Le Carre

ISBN: 978-1-910575-48-2

You can discover more information about Georgia Le Carre and future releases here.

https://www.facebook.com/georgia.lecarre
https://twitter.com/georgiaLeCarre
http://www.goodreads.com/GeorgiaLeCarre

Appreciations

I wish to extend my deepest and most profound gratitude to:

Caryl Milton
Elizabeth Burns
Nicola Rhead
Shannon Lee
Tracy Gray
Brittany Urbaniak

Author Note

The town of Durango Falls cannot be found on an ordinary American map.
It only exists in Georgia's mind!
:-)

Contents

"To draw you must close your eyes and sing."

-Pablo Picasso.

One

Lara

https://www.youtube.com/watch?v=a33sB3ck28A

I pushed open the heavy wooden door of Durango Falls' library and stepped into the still, hushed space. Other than my sculpting studio, this was without a doubt my favorite place. I came here almost every day. I think I loved the smell of old books mixed with pine floor cleaner and the lovely echo inside mostly empty, large stone buildings.

At this time of day there was usually no one around. I heard the water cooler gurgle in the left-hand corner of the room, and the lazy whirling sound the machinery inside the old heaters made. I shook the snow off my cap, peeled my thick gloves off, and stuffed them into my coat pockets. Swiping my white cane in smooth arcs in front of me, I took the twelve steps to the front desk.

Hannah Heinberger was usually on duty on Wednesday afternoons, but from her perfume, sage and roses, I knew that Elaine was manning the desk today. They must have swapped shifts.

"Hey, Elaine," I greeted as I reached her.

"Ooo ... just the person I wanted to see," she said.

I could tell immediately that she was bursting with some piece of juicy gossip. It was funny how Elaine could always find salacious rumors in a town with a population of less than a thousand. Notorious gossip or not, she had a heart of gold and I could not remember a time when we were not best friends.

I laid my left hand at the edge of the counter. Whatever the news was it had Elaine all fired up. She was almost bubbling over with excitement.

"What is it?" I asked curiously.

She leaned forward, disturbing the air. Her breath, she's been eating peanut butter cookies, was warm on my cold cheeks. "You'll never guess who came in here this morning," she cried triumphantly.

I kept my face straight. "Beyonce?"

"Fine. I just won't tell you, and you'll just miss the juiciest piece of information this town has heard in twenty years," she huffed, irritated that I had spoilt her surprise. I mean, who could she come up with better than Beyonce?

I grinned evilly. "Fine. I'm sure I'll hear from Emma Jean."

"I haven't told her yet," she said with great satisfaction.

"Elaine Crockett, I might miss the juiciest piece of information this town has heard in twenty years if you don't tell me, but you're going to burst if you don't spill the beans."

"Kit Carson," she blurted out instantly.

"Kit Carson," I echoed, surprised. Well, well, this time she did have a juicy bit between her teeth.

Every small town had a loner, a mysterious, gruff, elusive, anti-social person who refused to be part of the community. Kit Carson was this town's ghost. He lived on a large track of wooded land that he had converted into some kind of wolf sanctuary. Occasionally, he would drive into town in his pickup truck, but he wouldn't make eye-contact or speak to anyone other than to grunt.

I heard he was a hulk: six feet seven inches tall and as solid as a brick house, but that he walked with a slight limp and had a scarred face that nobody actually got a good look at.

Funny thing about Kit Carson was he'd turned the tables on our tiny town. We didn't take kindly to outside folk. You could live within our midst for fifty years and still be considered an outsider. Kit Carson was not born and raised local, and coming on his own like that without knowing a soul in our town, he was just plain asking for trouble.

He came to Durango Falls when I was about seventeen years old, and I would be twenty-two in July. So he'd been around for five years now, and even though our men folk have tried to extend the hand of friendship to him, he outright refused to have anything to do with us except for the commercial kind.

Two years ago Casey Goodnight said she saw dog tags peep out of his shirt while he was paying for steel cables at the hardware store. Yes sir, that sure gave the whole town something to gossip about. Coffee mornings weren't the same for weeks after.

With falsely sweet voices the good town folk picked apart the man's "secret". Obviously, he had been dishonorably discharged from the army, and it was pure shame that made him avoid contact with the rest of humanity and turn his back on God. Yes, that's right, Kit Carson had never seen the inside of our Church. Naturally, he had no wife because what God fearing woman would want such a heathen?

Although, with time that last piece of gossip morphed to – he murdered her. People said they heard the wolves howling on full moon nights while they were passing at the edge of his land. The stories about him got weirder and weirder. Some of them were downright crazy. Serial killer stuff. I guess we had some very bored folk in our town and they made up their own entertainment.

"Yup," Elaine said in the same voice she employed to report scandals, "the man strode in here this morning bigger than a tree, stuck up a piece of paper on the Job's Board, and left. Not a word to anyone."

"Wow," I whispered. "What's he looking for?" I thought she would say foreman, or housekeeper.

She took a deep breath.

"What?" I prompted, inexplicably intrigued by the mystery of it all.

"You ready for this?"

Two

Lara

"Maybe it's better if I read it to you." I heard her rustling a bit with a piece of paper. "Right. Here we are." She paused dramatically. "Blind Reader Wanted. Twice a week. Only females need apply. Kit Carson." She paused again. "There is a phone number underneath."

I shut my open mouth. I couldn't have heard right. "Did you say blind reader?"

"That's what it says here."

"What the hell is a blind reader?"

"A blind person who reads, I reckon."

I frowned. "What on earth would he want a blind reader for?"

"Here's what I think," Elaine whispered. "I think he's ashamed of his scars. I think he doesn't want anybody seeing them." She caught a quick breath. "I think you should apply."

"What? No. Are you mad? That advert is just weird."

"Don't be silly. The man's not dangerous. He's just anti-social."

"Not dangerous! Aren't you the one who said he killed his wife and buried her in the woods and the wolves are there so no one goes looking for her bones?"

She giggled. “Well, I was bored that afternoon. Don’t you think it’ll be fun?”

“You just want me to apply so you’d have all kinds of new gossip to spread around.”

“What a thing to say. As if I’d do that to you. I’d apply if I were blind.”

“No you wouldn’t.”

“Yes, I would,” she insisted.

“Since when?” I demanded.

“If he’d only look at me, I’d do him. The body on the man. He’s so hot I wouldn’t mind melting on him.”

“Jesus, Elaine.”

“Anyway, you should totally apply, Lara. I mean, I’ll drive you there and sit in his living room and wait while you read for the man. So you’ll be totally safe. It’ll be fun. At the very least it’ll be interesting. Please, Lara. Have a heart. I’m dying of boredom here.”

“I knew it. You just want new gossip.”

“Come on. I’d ask someone else, but you’re the only blind person in town.”

“Isn’t Mrs. Murtle blind too?”

“That old biddie,” she dismissed immediately. “She’s about to keel over any moment. I heard her sons have already dug her grave.”

I shook my head in wonder at that untrue piece of gossip.

“Besides, it’ll do my eyes good. Man candy always does, especially the mysterious brooding kind.”

I laughed. “I didn’t know you were perving on him.”

"I am," she admitted. "So are you going to do it or not?"

"I don't know, Elaine. It's awkward."

"Look, if you don't apply, I'm going to poke my eyes out and apply myself," she growled.

I laughed. "I'll think about it."

"Call him now."

"Oh, hell."

Fast as lightning she dipped her hand into my purse and extracted my cellphone. Before I could protest I heard her dialing.

"Elaine," I cried out as a ringing tone sounded.

It echoed in the silence of the library and how weird, but I felt my heart suddenly become still. As if something important was about to happen. Elaine thrust the phone into my hand. I took it in a daze and brought it to my ear. It felt as if I had waited my whole life for that moment, and finally it was there. I exhaled the breath I was holding.

"Mr. Carson?" I croaked.

"Speaking." His voice was deep and smooth, but wary.

"My name is Lara Young and I'm ... um ... calling about the ... uh ... reading job. Can you tell me a bit more about it?"

"Are you blind?"

I blinked with the directness of his question. "Well, I don't carry a white cane around for fun."

"Fine. I'll go through the job spec when I see you. When are you able to come to my home?"

"Er ..."

"Tomorrow at nine o'clock," Elaine whispered in my other ear.

"Tomorrow at nine in the morning," I told him.

"Do you know the address?" he asked abruptly.

Elaine tapped on my hand to indicate that she did. "Yes."

"Nine," he said and rang off.

I put my cellphone back into my purse, still in a daze.

"Isn't this exciting?" Elaine asked with a giggle.

Three

Kit

The moon was full and the reflection of its light off the newly-fallen snow lit up the house almost as bright as daylight. I liked these cold, still nights when the moon was high and full. Rather than try to go to sleep and miss the magic, I always hung out on the front porch with my wolves.

I watched them as they moved in the otherworldly light, their eyes glowing a feverish green and their thick coats glistening with health. The strong muscles underneath were clearly defined: a testament to their impressive power. They were restless, as they always were during full moon.

As I was...

I saw Koa, the biggest of the pack lift his nose to the sky and howl, long and deep, a wild cry that still had the ability to give me chills, even after all this time. One by one the others followed. I closed my eyes and let their haunting calls caress my skin and move through me. It awakened ancient memories, old spirits, sleeping shadows. And there were many of those buried in the graveyard of my soul.

When I first wound up at the edge of this mountain I was a fucking mess. Driven nearly mad with the raw brutality and senseless violence

I had seen in the Military, I was a disaster waiting to happen. Like one of those tortured men, who got himself a gun, walked into a shopping complex, and blasted everyone, man, woman, and child away, thinking they were doing them a favor, because the world was so fucking irredeemably ugly.

PTSD. Awww ... looked like it should be a box with a pretty red ribbon around it. I'll tell you what it is. It was raw screams that infected every damn thought you had during the day, and chased you into your dreams. You woke up screaming, tearing at your own hair. I began to question everything about humanity. Even my *own*.

Yeah, I thought about putting the barrel of a gun into my mouth.

Only the image of my mother in her house surrounded by her white picket fence house and flag flying proudly in her immaculate yard kept my brains from splattering out behind me.

I had two options: Dive into therapy and deal with all the things I had seen, or get the hell out of dodge and hide from the stupid idea of confronting the nightmare. Only an idiot could come up with such a shit idea – how did one confront what I had seen? The innocent children blown to bits, your mate's steaming guts in your bare hands.

Guess which option I took?

They gave me meds and wished me luck. What a fucking laugh! The plan was simple. Withdraw from it all for a while. I got into my pickup and began driving, away from anyone and anything I knew. Crossed two state lines and would have driven right through Durango Falls too. Not in a million years would I have dreamed of staying in it. A town forgotten by time.

Fuck, I could smell the backstabbing, fake, two-faced judgmental breeders. I had lived in a small town like that when I was a kid. I knew all about their small-time gossip, their nasty little secrets, and the incestuous bonds between them all. It was the kind of place I'd rather die than live in.

But thirty minutes out of town and I saw a sign:

For Rent Or Sale
Old Man's Creek
House and all thirty acres!

Thirty acres! The road was snarled up with weeds so I couldn't even drive into it. I had to get out of my pickup and walk up the long, rutted road.

It was more of a goat's trail than a road.

But it was also summer, and it was gloriously beautiful: the land, the creek, the forest behind it, even the old house in its sad state of disrepair called to me. I rubbed the dirt from one of the glass panes and looked in through the window. It was all wood, with a big stone fireplace, sparsely furnished, and perfect for my needs, but most of all it was so remote and isolated I knew that it was the right spot to waste my life for a couple of weeks. Out here I could hunt and fish and recover. Get my head straight before I moved on.

As I walked around the property, clearing overgrown creepers and brambles out of my way, it never even crossed my mind that I'd make a life here, but a couple of weeks turned into a month. I felt a new vigor come into my body. There is nothing like hard, physical labor and living off the land to heal a man's body.

I flushed the head meds down the toilet.

One month slipped into another, and soon the forest was changing into golds, russets, and browns. No amount of books, Youtube videos, websites, documentaries, or award winning photographs could have prepared me for the beauty of what appeared before my eyes. Even as I immersed myself in the spectacular blaze of color, I knew I was facing down a harsh winter on my own. However hard life was, it would be ten times harder once the snows came.

I had to make a decision: stay or go? I decided to wait just until the show was over, last leaves had fallen away, and the first layer of snow had drifted in. After that I would go.

The real truth was I was waiting for the snow because I wanted to see the tracks of the creatures that I knew were playing a game of hide and seek with me on my hiking expeditions. I sensed that they were close, a hunch, a side effect of war, but they never revealed themselves to me.

I chopped six cords of wood, covered them under a tarp, and waited for the first snow to come. I didn't have long to wait. Overnight it blanketed the ground in white, hushed the air, and changed the landscape into a Christmas picture card.

I packed a bag and left early.

Four

Kit

The pre-dawn forest was a wonderland of freshly fallen snow. The spruces stood tall and black against the sky, and the complete stillness was disturbed only occasionally by a Raven's caw, or the sound of a twig breaking with the weight of the snow. My breath formed ice crystals on the fur rimming my hood.

In the pale light, for the first time since I moved into Durango Falls, I saw their tracks. I crouched down to study them. Wolves! Big ones.

In an instant their paw prints changed everything. I was no longer a soldier so sick with what I had witnessed I had to hide at the edge of some godforsaken town. I was suddenly taken back in time, a century back. I was standing in the land of the men who had come in covered wagons, the settlers and explorers, of the old West.

If their lurid tales of killer predators were to be believed, I was looking at a short, unequal scuffle on the snow before it was all over. My bones would become part of the forest, and no one would know better. They'd just think I'd packed up, and gone back to wherever I had come from.

As I hiked along the tree line I realized I was being watched ... stalked. A lone, dark shadow was moving slowly along the frozen ground. Without warning the shadow broke from cover.

A huge midnight-black timber wolf.

His hide gleamed in the pale light. He headed towards me, running with the loping, loose-jointed grace of his kind.

I stopped, slipped off my pack and waited. My breath came in quick, shallow gasps. A hundred yards away he stopped, raised his head, and tried to get my wind. The air was still, so he wove through the trees, then stopped again, and looked at me.

The great beast was close enough for me to see his eyes: bright yellow and penetrating. He stood tense and alert, but made neither movement nor sound. We stood watching each other. It was weird, but I felt as if I knew him. From another lifetime. Or another realm.

I saw him for what he was: a guardian of the land. He had a timeless understanding of the mountain, the forest, the land, and the seasons. It was the kind of intelligence that was rare even for some humans.

Humans thought fewer wolves meant more deer, that no wolves would mean a hunter's paradise, but without wolves, the unchecked deer population will eat a mountain into barren ground, a lush prairie into a dust bowl.

There was a cracking sound in the woods, and the black beast whirled away, and disappeared soundlessly into the shadows. From that moment on I knew I would be staying for good. I had some money saved so I bought Old Man's Creek, which of course, turned out to be the best decision I ever made. If I hadn't stayed, Adam would have died.

Adam was my first.

That was the year the bears had woken up early and the berries were late. They were hungry. If you left a bowl of fruit out where it could be seen through a window, a bear would come fucking crashing through your walls as if wood logs were nothing more than cardboard. I almost had to put a couple of rounds into a black bear that year, they were so aggressive.

Adam was only a pup then. He couldn't have been more than a couple of years old. Badly mauled by a bear, abandoned by his pack (yeah, the animal world is nearly as cruel as ours), and barely able to drag his mangled bloody body, he miraculously made it all the way to my backyard.

He was damn near dead when I carried him back in. I put him on a bit of blanket on my kitchen floor, and he looked into my eyes. I knew then he had no fight left in him. He was ready to die. In his dim stare there was no anger, violence, or even a clawing desire to hang on. There was only an acceptance of his impending demise.

In a strange way it was like looking at a deeper, wiser portion of my own soul. That part of me that knew. Nothing was permanent. All must wither away and die.

Fuck withering away and dying. He was only a pup. I'd be damned before I let him die on me. Back then I didn't know much about wolves, and the roads were so bad I couldn't even rush him to a vet, but I knew how to wash a cut and bandage a limb. Hell, I had more experience with that than I cared to remember. I made a teat out of a plastic bag and dripped warm milk into his mouth.

It didn't take long to gain his trust.

Over the next few weeks I nursed him back to health, or what I thought was pretty close to it. Angry scars covered his back and side, and one of his legs never worked right again even though I was sure it wasn't broken. In spite of that I watched him grow stronger and bolder day by day.

He began to wander further and further away from the house. I was certain by the time the spring winds came, he would vanish. Instead, he started sleeping on the porch. When he came up the stairs, jumped on my bed, and washed my face with enough saliva to wet a cat, I knew he would stay.

I named him Adam because he was first, but others would come after him. As they have. One by one they joined the tribe and I've named each one. It's important to me to get to know all of them. They are my family. In fact, they are the only company I keep these days.

Until today, when I spoke to Lara Young.

She had a sweet voice. Musical. I could almost imagine her laughing. She sounded young too. Almost childlike. And yet she had enough sass to burn down a house. *I don't carry a white stick around for fun.*

Ha, ha. I smiled. I used to like them fiery. Once, when I was still a man looking for a woman. My mind wandered off to what she looked like, and then pulled myself up short. What the fuck was I thinking of? I didn't want a woman. I certainly didn't want a relationship. I knew only too well what humans were capable of. Lies. Deceit. Murder. Corruption. Manipulation. Greed. Cruelty.

The list was endless.

The people I trusted could be counted on one hand.

Why? Why did I put that job advert up? Who the fuck really knows?

I was dreaming of a time past when my mother read to me.

I was lonely.

I wanted to look at a woman who could not see me staring at her.

I wanted to be with another human being who could not see my scars.

I wanted to hear a woman's voice in my empty house.

Maybe I wanted to know if I could still act like a normal man around a woman after living for years with only wolves for company.

I thought of old Andak wandering around the fields out back – he was one of my oldest wolves, probably the wisest. He was also almost blind. How carefully he moves along the fencerow, letting his nose do most of the work. His sense of smell was so heightened he was sharper than wolves much fitter and younger than him.

I thought of Lara Young. What would she sense with her heightened awareness?

Five

Lara

I knew the moon was whole that night because the air always became full of something unknown every time it did. Often, I could even feel the strange and precious magic running like wild fire in my veins. It poured out of my fingertips as I worked my art. Like a woman possessed I worked until the early morning hours, creating things that I packed and shipped off to a gallery in New York.

In the beginning, I didn't tell Sasha Smirnov, the owner of the gallery, that I was blind. I wanted people to buy my pieces because they were beautiful, and thought provoking, not because they were created by an artist with a "condition".

I didn't want to be indulged.

I wanted to be judged like everybody else. As far as I was concerned, blindness to an artist was not disability or a disability to be pitied. It was an advantage to be envied. I think the thing that shocked Sasha the most was my use of colors.

"Does someone tell you which colors to use?" he asked, circling me restlessly as I worked on my sculpture.

"No."

"Have you ever been able to see?"

"I was born blind."

"But how do you know colors if you have never seen them?' he asked, baffled.

"I feel them, by smell and texture."

"The colors smell different?" he asked, astonished.

"Absolutely."

He stood behind me and watched me work for a whole day, but he left for New York none the wiser. I suppose it must be impossible for those with sight to comprehend a life based not on what your eyes tell you, but what your other senses show you.

He couldn't understand that the images in my brain were no less vivid than those in the world he lived in. He assumed that I lived in terrible darkness. He was shocked when I told him my blindness was a gift. I'm better blind. I'm blessed. My art is more beautiful because I can't see.

"Don't you want to see?" he asked incredulously.

I chewed my bottom lip. To be perfectly honest no one had ever asked me that before. "I don't know," I told him truthfully.

"Why not? If someone asked if me I wanted to experience something new, I'd say, yes." He seemed genuinely perplexed.

I thought about his statement carefully. "But what if you had to give up something very precious to you to have that experience?"

He couldn't figure out what I was talking about. "What do you have to give up?" he asked incredulously.

It was impossible to explain. Depth, motion, perspective, vantage point, surfaces, contours, edges, and other characteristics that sighted people seem to completely miss. When I touch a piece of wood, it talks to me. I don't see it as a piece of wood.

No one else in my family was blind so when I was young people would pity me a lot, but they shouldn't have. Since I had never experienced sight, it had no physical, psychological, or social meaning. As a child I wasn't even aware that I was without sight.

I ran down the stairs, swam, played in the garden, ate, talked, fought with my brother. I was constantly bumping into walls and furniture, and always wore a collection of bruises in different stages of healing. My mother said I'd fall, and if I wasn't hurt too badly, I would pick myself up and run off into my next adventure totally unaware what the fuss was all about.

When I grew older I learned that the world was designed for people with sight. My mother taught me that it could take me twice as long, but I could always do whatever I wanted.

When it was time for me to go to a school, my mother told me I was too special for a little school like the one we had in Durango Falls. She was adamant she would teach me herself.

After she died many years later, I found her diaries, and had them all translated into braille. That was when I realized that she had homeschooled me because she was afraid the other kids would snatch away my guide cane, steal my lunch, make fun of me ... Actually, the list of misfortunes that she thought could befall me were literally endless.

It made my eyes well with tears to know how frightened she had been for me, but how wise she was never to let even a single one of her fears infect me. It allowed me to trust fearlessly. Even when I had no reason to, I simply trusted and never stopped believing in myself.

Nobody believed I could ride, but I trusted my horse and she put wings on my back. She went from giddy up to breakneck speed real fast, but I just hung on like a tick, the wind in my hair, and the knowledge buried in my heart that I could lasso the moon if I really, really tried. When she came to a sudden halt I went flying into the air, but I landed well so that was okay too.

When we were young Elaine would do that thing with the puddles, where she would shout, "puddle" while we were out walking and I would jump to avoid stepping into it.

Sometimes she would shout puddle even though there was no puddle. I would jump and she would laugh at me. It should have made me angry, but it didn't. I liked to hear her laugh.

When you trust, good things happen.

Six

Kit

I fought the sheets like a wild dog caught in a trap all night long, and woke up before dawn. The brilliant full moon had sunk beyond the trees and the room was filled with blue light. I was restless and excited. My stomach felt like a dark pit filled with twisting snakes.

For the first time since I arrived at Old Man's Creek another human being was going to be in my space! I was about to have a visitor. Problem was I didn't know if I could still interact properly with one of my kind anymore. I was used to listening to nothing but the sound of my own heart and the wild critters around me.

"It's your own damn fault," I grumbled to myself.

I'd even taken to talking to myself. Pushing back the blanket, I realized the house was cold. Far too bitter for a young lady. I jackknifed out of bed, got dressed quickly, and went downstairs.

Downstairs it was dark and cold. Like the wolves I had got used to the cold, but it would be nice to light a fire. I hadn't lit a fire since last winter. I opened the front door and went out into the frosty morning air. Andak was curled by the porch chair. He raised his old bones and came to sniff my hand. I rubbed his head.

"You better be on your best behavior cause we're having a visitor come around, old boy," I said to him.

Chepi, a young female, and the latest addition to the pack, bounded next to me as I walked to the shack. I stopped to watch her playfully roll on the snow. She was inviting me to rub her belly. Of all the wolves, she was the closest to me. Sometimes she behaved more like a pet dog than a wolf.

I obliged before filling my arms with firewood. Back in the house, I cleaned out the fireplace and made sure the chimney was clear, then I lay down tinder, made a grid of the kindling, and finally arranged the logs using an old Indian trick that maximized air flow.

I sniffed the air. I thought it smelled okay, but it was entirely possible that I had become immune to the smell of wolf and unwashed man. From the cupboard under the sink I took out dusters, cloths, cleaning sprays, a bucket and a mop.

For the next hour, I dusted, vacuumed, wiped, and polished like a demon. The time passed quickly and the mundane activity made the tight knot in my chest go away. I stood back, looked at my living room and felt pleased with myself. The place was cleaner than it had ever been. All traces of fur were gone, and the floor was polished to a high shine with some kind of lemon wax.

I sniffed the air again.

Better.

I did the hallway in a third of the time and moved to the kitchen. Pale yellow sunlight was filtering through the trees when I finished. I started to put away the things.

Toilet?

What if she wanted to use the toilet? Taking out the cleaning stuff again, I gave that a good cleaning. Made the taps shine like a mirror before I realized she wouldn't be able to see them.

I went back into the living room and crouched in front of the fireplace. I lit the tinder using lighter fluid, and watched the fire crackle and roar into life, from the center outward.

With it burning merrily, I fitted the fire guard and stood. The entire house would be toasty and warm in a couple of hours. I took the stairs two at a time and made for the shower. The water was freezing cold, like needles on my skin. I came out refreshed and stood in front of the mirror. My skin was red and I had a flash of when the explosion happened.

A white flash.

I didn't hurt at all.

Afterwards, lying in a hospital bed in Kandahar. Third degree burns on forty percent of my body, the skin on the right side of my face hanging in tatters. It hurt like fuck then. Oh fuck did it hurt. I screamed like a stuck pig.

I touched my face. The scars weren't bad enough to scare little kids, thank God for that, but they were bad enough that they made them stare and point. Bad enough that I never, ever forgot they were there. And worse, I would never forget *how* they *got* there.

I turned away from the mirror, scowling. What the fuck was the matter with me? It was years since I allowed my mind to dwell on the past. I got dressed in clean clothes and went downstairs. The fire was doing nicely, and the house felt warm, and smelled clean. I went out to the porch. The air was frozen. My breath came up in puffs. I clenched and unclenched my hands nervously. Strange, that I should be so wired up about a woman coming to my house. I haven't given a shit what people think of me since I was a kid.

Chepi lifted her head off the floor, turned it toward the road, and perked up her ears. When it came to an unbelievable sense of hearing, nothing in this world could beat a wolf. An old Indian friend of mine told me that wolves could hear as far as ten miles away out in the open, and their hearing was spades greater than that of most dogs. I can vouch for that, as I've seen them alert to a vehicle well over fifteen minutes before it actually passes the turning into the dirt road.

In other words, my wolves serve as the best security system I could possibly have.

Sure enough, a few minutes later I watched an old blue Toyota drive slowly down the road. The three wolves near the fence hauled themselves up and sauntered around the back of the house, towards the hill beyond. They almost always made themselves scarce when someone ventured this way. Usually it was someone lost and seeking directions.

The car stopped halfway up the dirt road.

My body was still, but my heart was beating a little too fast and my mind was in overdrive: she had changed her mind. She wasn't coming up to the house. I didn't realize until that moment just how much I'd been looking forward to her arrival. Acute disappointment filled every cell in my body.

Crushed, I sagged against the pillar.

Seven

Lara

To reach the house we had driven nearly half an hour out of the town.

"Well, son of a biscuit," Elaine exclaimed suddenly and stopped the car. We had just left the smooth paved road and turned down a dirt road filled with pot holes.

"What? What's wrong?" I asked worriedly.

"The house just came into view."

"And?"

She turned towards me. "I think this might have been a really bad idea, Lara."

"Why?"

"It looks like a fricking haunted house."

Calmly, I wound down the glass and inhaled the air. It was full of the fresh scent of pine trees, snow, and something else. Something that called to me.

"Describe the house to me," I said.

"Look, Lara. I know I talked you into taking this job, but I honestly don't think you should go inside that house. It's giving me the creeps."

"Please, Elaine. Just describe it to me."

"Okay. It's an old turn of the century two story. It's nestled in a bunch of trees and it backs onto a proper forest."

"Does it have a wide porch?"

"How the hell do you do that?"

I smiled. "I told you before it's like a shape in my mind. Scientists say that I'm actually accessing the same area of the brain that you are when you are looking at something with your eyes."

"I don't know what you're looking at in your brain, but I'm looking at a haunted house."

"It's not haunted. It's just very lonely. I want to keep my appointment."

"I think you're making a big mistake," she warned.

"I'm not," I said firmly, and wound the glass back up.

Elaine started the car. "Just so you know, I'm not coming in. I'll wait for you outside."

The car jolted over rough gravel and pot holes in the road. "That'll be fine."

"If anything happens you scream as loud as you can and I'll drive back to town as fast as I can, and tell everybody, all right?"

I laughed. "Thanks, Elaine. That's real comforting to know."

"Don't be taking that tone with me, girl. You're going in against my better judgement."

"Is he standing on the porch?"

For a while there was silence as she peered through the windscreen. "Oh, my God! Yes. He is. Did you see that in that brain of yours too?"

"Nah. It was just a guess."

Eight

Kit

The old car moved closer, jolting crazily over the holes in the road. My body tightened. It wasn't nerves – it was my survival instinct kicking in. Military training never died, and any new situation put me right back into the defensive zone.

I'm sure my therapists would have something to say about that, but my blind reader was here and my body was preparing to meet her. The car skidded dangerously to a stop.

A woman wearing dark glasses stepped out of the car, half-turned toward the house, and ... the peace of the morning air shattered. Blood slammed into my brain, and alarm bells flared as I stared in shock.

I knew she was young, I could tell by her voice, but I never counted on her being drop-dead gorgeous. Fucking hell. She looked like she had stepped out of the pages of a fancy magazine. My breathing was ragged. I didn't really think about what I was expecting, but not this. Not this. This girl was special. Too special for me ... but fuck me, if I didn't want her the way I wanted nothing else in my life. I wanted to make her mine and never let her go.

I gripped the railing and watched her come up the drive, her cane making even swipes on the ground, her steps purposeful and unfaltering. Her long honey curls bounced with every step. She was wearing a knit cap and blue coat, but it was unbuttoned and boy, did she have curves. Her cat-like face was filled with concentration, and her nose was a cute little button dotted with freckles, but I knew that when she smiled she would be lethal.

I caught a movement out of the corner of my eye. It was one of the younger wolves, Thomas. I found him in the forest eighteen months ago caught in a trap yelping and crying in agony. His poor leg was broken. I tranquilized him, carried him back here, and nursed him back to health. He didn't need to be persuaded to join my pack. Now he was stalking the girl up the driveway, pausing every time she did, taking his time to get a closer look.

Hell, I understood that.

I wanted a closer look too!

Amazingly, she knew the wolf was following her. She stopped and turned her head ever-so-slightly. Her attitude and motion hardly changed, but she was totally attuned to the sounds the wolf was making. I've been out there among the wolves, and believe me, when they want to be silent, they certainly know how to be. But no matter how quiet Thomas was, she could hear him.

Huh. Interesting.

And then she was at the bottom of the steps. I wasn't sure what to do. Go down and help her? Just stand there? Say something?

"I can hear you breathing," she said, and smiled at me.

And damned if that smile didn't light up her face like a lightbulb and transform it into something even more beautiful than what it already was ... if such a thing were even possible.

My stomach did a single, lazy somersault. "Hello," I said stupidly. It was all that came to mind. My voice sounded husky and strange.

"Hello, Mr. Carson. I'm Lara." She held out her hand, her smile growing larger.

I quickly stepped forwards and clattered down the steps as clumsy as bigfoot himself. She didn't wear gloves even though the air was frigid. I grasped her hand inside mine. It was small and delicate. I don't think I had ever held such a fine hand before. Her skin was so lovely and warm it made my insides turn to mush.

I wanted to hold her hand forever. What the fuck! I yanked my hand away.

Her smile faltered, and there was a part of me that was happy I didn't linger and let her know how much I wanted to hold onto her soft skin, but another part of me felt bad about making her doubt herself. I glanced at the woman still sitting in the car. She had her neck craned forward and was staring at us through the windscreen with bug eyes. "Is your friend going to wait in the car?"

She grinned. "She'll come in when she gets too cold ... or too curious."

I nodded and realized that she could not see my nod. “Right. There are four steps up to the porch.”

She made no move to go up the steps. Was she waiting for me to move? Or was I supposed to take her hand and lead her up? I rubbed my cheek uncertainly. How the hell did one deal with a blind woman? I sure as hell didn’t want to insult her.

“You go ahead of me, and I’ll follow. I’m very good at tracing sounds and getting to where I need to be,” she said into the awkward silence.

That settled that. I went up the steps and walked to the front door. Glancing behind to make sure she was following, I opened it, stepped in, and held it for her so she could come through. She moved confidently, barely hesitating at the threshold. I watched as she moved through and stood in the hallway, listening ... and like the wolves smelling the air.

“Uh, there’s a fire in the living room. Would you prefer to sit in there? Or we can sit at the kitchen table,” I offered.

“By the fire sounds lovely,” she said softly.

“Would you like me to take your coat?” I asked, going closer to her. She smelled of fruit. Some sort of berry. It was coming from her lips. Man, I was so fucked.

“Thank you, but I think I’ll keep it on for a little while,” she replied.

“This way,” I said, and passed her in the narrow space. Almost touching, there was only an inch between her round breasts and my midriff.

My cock twitched and hardened. Jesus! I haven't had sex for too fucking long.

I led the way into the living room. It felt too warm, or maybe it was just me. I fingered my collar. A trickle of sweat ran down my back. I was dying to take my sweater off. I walked to a chair that stood between her and my most comfortable armchair by the fire and yanked it out of her way. It made a scraping sound on the wood. I stood next to the armchair and called, "Over here."

I watched her work her way over to me, her cane moving in small half-circles. When it caught on the rug she paused then continued once she had figured out it was the edge of the rug. She reached the chair and felt it with her hands, before lowering herself with an almost regal air.

"Thank you," she said, and there was that smile again.

My stomach did another slow somersault. That was when I started to think that maybe this was all a big mistake. Until now my life was without complication. Me and my wolves.

No one had penetrated my walls ever, tried to psychoanalyze me, or peer into the dark depths of my melting pot of loathing, self-hate, pain, guilt and shame.

Now all of a sudden the walls that I thought were impenetrable to other human beings were looking like they were made of ice and someone had just taken an icepick to them.

Nine

Lara

When I got out of the car, I didn't know what I would find at the house, but something magnetic and mysterious that simply would not be denied called to me. So I did what I always do.

I jumped in with both feet.

As I walked towards him, I smelled the animal that was shadowing me and I knew it was not a dog, so I guessed it must be one of his wolves. He meant me no harm. That much was obvious. I carried on walking. There was ice on the ground and I concentrated on not landing on my butt on the snow. His wolves must have lain on the porch only minutes ago because their scent hung strong in the air. Then he came down the step, his gait was that of a prowling animal, full of coiled energy and fluid. I scented the leather of his footwear, the heat rising from his freshly washed skin, and the odors that lay underneath his skin.

Good god, he was more animal than man!

Kit Carson was definitely ... intriguing.

I could gauge that he was more than a foot taller than me. And he was broad. Very broad. And strong. Powerful vibes came off him. This was a man who knew how to use an axe. He took my hand in his and it was as big as my face. And full of strength. One swipe ...

He showed me to his living room. It was small, hot as a furnace, and smelled of wax polish and burning wood. He called me to sit in the best armchair in the room, but it had a broken spring. It jagged my butt, and I shifted slightly. I didn't think he would notice, but he must have because he shuffled uncomfortably, then moved to the other end of the room. I heard a creak as his weight settled down in a chair. I heard his clothes rustle as he leaned forward.

Well ... this should be interesting.

I started to peel off my coat, and heard a sharp intake of breath.

"Is everything all right?" I asked, frowning, my senses heightened. Suddenly, there was no sound in the room except the fire crackling. I breathed in the smell of wood smoke and waited.

"Yes," he said harshly. "Fine."

That bitter voice might have frightened a lesser woman. Not me. I believed in him implicitly. The tense muscles in my body relaxed. I knew I had nothing to fear from him. I was wearing my good black trousers so I crossed my legs confidently.

"You've built quite a fire. Not many people know how to get a proper one going," I said conversationally.

He grunted.

Undaunted by his lack of response, I persisted at polite conversation. "So you'd like me to read to you?"

"Yes," he said gruffly.

"Why did you particularly want a blind reader?"

"I don't like people looking at me," he muttered, his voice so low it was almost inaudible. His foot tapped restlessly on the ground. He was wearing heavy duty boots. I imagined them to be badly scuffed.

He was tough and rugged and gruff and annoyed, but underneath all that bluster was a lot of anxiety. This was a man who for whatever reason had chosen to hide away from the world, but now that the world had come to his doorstep – in the form of a woman he himself had conjured up with an ad, of all things. Some part of him stood amazed by what he had done.

"I see," I said softly.

"I have a book for you to start reading." He paused, fidgeted nervously, then rushed on, endearingly, I thought. "Assuming you want the job, that is."

I thought of him as a bear. A big grizzly. Dangerous, but somehow I knew I was safe with him. "Before I begin, we should discuss terms, shouldn't we?" I asked gently.

"Terms?" he repeated. He seemed unprepared and startled.

"Of course. For instance, how often would you like me to read to you? I run a small business." I re-arranged my coat on my knees. "I'm a sculptor, but my hours are quite flexible."

"Uh ... twice a week?"

"Okay." I waited, but he remained silent. "And for how long? How long do you expect each session to be?"

I heard him scratch his face, or his head. "Oh! Umm. Maybe one hour each time?"

I nodded. “How much do you pay?”

“Oh.” He seemed genuinely dumbfounded. “How much would you like?”

I grinned cheekily. “I can name my price?”

“Within reason,” he said slowly. I was surprised to hear almost nothing more than his even breathing. He was adjusting to my approach and now he was calmly thinking things over. I was impressed with how quickly he could change and adapt. That spoke volumes about who he might be underneath all that gruff and grumble.

I crinkled my brow. I never thought I’d be deciding my own wage. He couldn’t have much money living here by himself, and I didn’t want to leave him out of pocket. My art paid for my expenses so I didn’t really need this job.

“Would $25.00 an hour work for you?” I asked.

As a sculptor who worked long hours without a single sound beyond the motion of my hands on the material, I had come to recognize the value in silence, but he stayed silent for so long I was about to reduce my wages to $20.00. Though it would not even have been worth my time, for some weird reason it felt important that I secure this job.

Just as I was about to open my mouth, he spoke again. “I’ll give you $50.00 an hour.”

My eyebrows rose with surprise. “I’m quite happy with $25.00.”

“$50.00 is a fair wage,” he insisted.

“All right. Thank you. There is one more problem. My friend drove me here, but I’m not sure that she will be willing to do it twice a week on a regular basis as it is thirty minutes each way to get here ...”

“I will pick you up,” he said immediately. I knew he was staring at me. I could feel his intense scrutiny as it moved over my body and face.

“Thank you,” I said.

“Where should I pick you up from?” he asked.

“How about meeting up at the Dairy Queen or in the library?”

“Library,” he said promptly. I should have known he wouldn’t want to hang around the Dairy Queen.

“What days would work for you?” I asked.

“I have no preference.”

“Tuesdays and Fridays?”

“Sure.”

I nodded. “How about two in the afternoon?”

“Yep.”

“Oh, and I nearly forgot.”

“What?” His voice was suddenly wary. This was a man who didn’t trust easy.

Ten

Lara

"Do you have any tea in your house?"

"Tea?" he echoed incredulously, as if I had said, poison.

I swallowed a smile. "Yes. Tea. You know, tea bags."

"I know what tea is." He sounded indignant. "No, I don't have any."

My smile broke through, anyway. Didn't surprise me in the least. He struck me as the type of man who would broker nothing less than coffee, black as night, and hot enough to burn.

"I love tea," I said conversationally.

"I don't have any tea," he repeated.

"Not yet you don't," I said, enjoying this little experiment in socializing a cross bear of a man who obviously hadn't dealt with another person in years. "But I hope you'll change that because I'd love to be offered a cup of tea each time I come to read to you. Perhaps you can consider it as part payment of our agreed fee. $49.00 plus a cup of tea."

He was entirely silent. Even his breath was gone. I waited – anyone who wants to play a game of words must understand the value of silence.

"You're not going to be easy because you're blind, are you?" he exhaled.

I gave him my broadest smile. "Honey, you have no idea."

"I'll get you the tea," he said, a mocking edge to his voice. "Although, you might need something stronger to soothe your nerves when you read the book I've got for you."

My stomach tightened. He was flirting with me! Who flirts with a blind girl? I had never flirted with anyone in my life. I didn't know how to. And yet with him, I felt bold and daring. I wanted to touch his face.

"Why?" I asked with a laugh. "Have you got naughty reading for the visually impaired?"

"Would you have minded if I did?"

"No. I've never read one so it'll be a new experience for me."

The fire crackled and spat. He didn't know what to say. It would seem I had turned him speechless.

One day, I promised myself I would unravel him, the way a playful kitten unravels a ball of wool. I listened to my heart beating in my chest.

"What kind of tea?" he asked quietly.

At that moment, a loud thump came from the back of the house. Kit immediately pushed his chair back and stood. His heavy footfalls went straight toward the sound. He walked out into the back of the house, where I presumed the kitchen was, and opened the back door. There was another thump, this one louder, as well as a high-pitched whine.

"Stop that," he scolded, his voice pitched so low it was almost a primitive growl.

Yes, he was definitely more animal than man. And sure enough, the thumps stopped. There was one more whine, this one almost resentful, and then the sound of rustling as whatever made the noise made a hasty retreat.

Kit returned to the room and sat down. I waited for an explanation the way a normal person would offer, but nothing was forthcoming.

"Oolong," I said.

"What?" he barked.

"Oolong tea. That's what I'd prefer."

"Okay."

I slipped my fingertips over my watch. How surprising. I'd already been in his house for twenty minutes. It was enough for one day. I placed my hands on the armchair rests and stood up. I heard him move. He moved swiftly, quietly. Like a man who had been trained in the art of fighting. "Thank you for meeting with me."

"You're ... you're not going to read today?"

I smiled. "You seem to be rather distracted and angry about something today. If you still want me to read to you, pick me up from the library on Friday."

Instinctively, I sensed his confusion. "Have I upset you? I don't get too many visitors so I'm a bit rough around the edges, but I mean you no harm," he explained.

"You've not upset me, Mr. Carson. I'm looking forward to Friday."

I took a step in the direction of the door, and he scrambled to get there before I did so he could open it for me. What a surprise – there was a gentleman underneath all that bluster and bluff. I paused at the threshold.

"You will let me look at you some day, won't you?"

"What?"

"With my hands." The idea intoxicated me. The pull from his body was so powerful the tiny hairs on my hands stood to attention.

"I have scars," he muttered.

"I know," I whispered. "Scars are not ugly to me. They are just shapes."

"Uh."

"So will you? Let me see you."

"Yes," his voice was husky.

"Until Friday," I said solemnly.

"Until tomorrow," he responded.

Then I turned away and made my way down the porch steps. Carefully, navigating my way down the driveway, I reached the car without incident, opened the passenger door and slipped inside. Before I could close the door Elaine pounced on me. "What happened in there? What took you so long?"

"Close that fly-attracting mouth of yours, Elaine. I've only been twenty minutes," I said, pulling at the seatbelt.

She snapped her mouth shut. "Well, it feels more like an hour. I was just about to break his door down to rescue you."

I laughed at the idea of I'll-wait-outside-for-you-Elaine breaking down Kit's door to rescue me. I loved her to death, but Elaine must be one of the biggest cowards on God's earth.

"Well?" she prompted.

“He was actually rather fascinating,” I said with a smile.

“Start right from the very beginning and don’t leave a single thing out,” she ordered as she reversed the car. And she made me spit out every detail too, as she drove us back to a life that wasn’t nearly as complicated or wonderful as the one being lived at Kit Carson’s abode.

Eleven

Kit

My heart was hammering as if it was about to fucking explode, and my dick was rock hard and pressing painfully against the zipper of my jeans. It felt as if all the blood in my body had rushed into my damn dick!

I was *aching* for her.

Never did a woman dressed in winter garb have such a devastating effect on me. My mind was racing with all kinds of thoughts. Not just any thoughts, but the kind of filthy fantasies I hadn't entertained since was a horny teenager.

I fucking lift her skirt.

She moans.

She's not wearing underwear.

I fucking spread her legs wide.

Yes, yes, she groans as my dick plunges into her wet pussy over and over again.

"Harder, Kit. Harder," she begs.

Oh, fuck it. What the hell? I wasn't going to walk around all day with this damn hard on. I found myself bounding upstairs to the bedroom. I sat on the bed, pulled my jeans down to my knees, and freed my cock. It sprung up like a Jack-in-the-Box. I lay back, closed my eyes, and visualized Lara naked. Not a stitch on that beautiful body.

She spread her legs and showed me her little cunt, decorated with soft blonde curls. It was so pretty I wanted to eat it.

"Let me suck you," she said, and opened her mouth.

I spat on my palm, gripped my shaft firmly, and began to stroke my hard cock.

I fed my cock to her hot, wet mouth. She took it greedily and moaned.

"Take me deeper," I ordered. Immediately, she deep-throated me, taking me all the way down her throat. I was twisting and excitedly fucking her mouth. Jesus, it felt so fucking awesome. I'd almost forgotten what a warm, soft, and eager mouth could do to a fully loaded cock in need of satisfaction.

I stroked the entire length of my shaft faster and faster. Pre-cum dripped from my engorged cock.

I leaned forward so I could suck on her deliciously rosy nipples.

"Are you going to fuck my tight pussy?" she asked.

"Oh, yes, sweet pea, I sure am"

I pulled out of her mouth and lay her face down on the bed. Her ass was in the air and her pussy peeked through. All and wet and begging for it. I plunged my bare cock into all that pinkness.

"Oh! fuck, Lara," I groaned, as my legs stiffened.

The build-up felt like flood water bursting through a dam. Nothing could contain it. Nothing. I exploded, shooting my hot load like a fountain into the air and covering my hands in a sticky mess. It had been so long since I'd cum like that.

My heart was hammering away, and my cock was still hard for her. I just lay and knew: This woman was going to be the death of me.

Twelve

Lara

My favorite book lay open in front of me, and my fingers moved steadily over the raised dots, but I read nothing. I checked my watch face for the fifth time. He still had five minutes before our appointed time to meet arrived.

I was sitting on a seat very close to the large windows facing west because it didn't manage to filter out all the sounds from the car park. I sighed and returned my fingers to the dots.

Two minutes later I heard the engine of an old truck stop outside. My heart started pounding. I placed my hands on my lap and listened carefully.

Old vehicles have an interesting sound, unhampered by computers or gadgets. An ancient vehicle that has been very well-maintained has an even more unique sound, somewhere between a roar and a purr. There is a solidness to it that fulfills the old saying: 'They don't make 'em like they used to.'

Kit's truck had that sound.

It was obviously very old, but lovingly cared for. A fact that didn't surprise me in the least. An old truck with a well-maintained engine seemed a perfect fit for what I knew about him so far.

What did surprise me was how different he was than during our first meeting.

"Hello, Lara," he said formally from a few feet away.

"Howdy doody to you too, Mr. Carson," I said with a grin.

"Shall we go?" I think I threw him some, but his voice was softer and friendly.

"Absolutely," I said, closing my book with a snap and standing up. "I'm always glad when I get to stop pretending to read."

He chuckled, the sound coming from deep within his chest.

The air around me moved as he turned.

"Do you say everything that comes into your head?" he asked as we walked towards the front door.

Our steps echoed in the empty space. "Mostly. Why?"

"Most people filter out the things that they think might embarrass themselves or others."

"Oh, I do too. You have no idea what I really thought when I first met you."

"See what I mean?"

"No, that doesn't count," I argued. "It would have if I'd actually told you what I was thinking."

He laughed again and held open the door.

"Good day, Hannah," I called out as we walked out into the freezing cold.

"Have a good night, Lara," her voice rang out as the door closed behind us.

I followed him to his truck. I sort of already knew where it was, but thought it best to let him lead. It wouldn't do to let him know I was literally stalking him by the window. He opened the door, and after feeling the height of the seat, I hopped in, as nimble as a goat. Well, that's what my Ma used to call me.

A stubborn, nimble goat.

The truck was toasty warm. The seats were wide and comfortable, and covered with butter-soft leather. I ran my palm over it as he got in beside me and closed the door. His arrival changed the air in the truck. Suddenly it was bristling with electricity. I wondered if he sensed it.

"I love old vehicles," I said, to quell the thousand butterflies fluttering in my stomach.

He paused. "How do you know it's old?"

"The sound of the engine." I grinned at him. "Don't tell me you can't hear all that gorgeousness purring away under the hood."

"Yes ma'am." His voice took on a note of pride. "I put a lot of time into this old girl."

"Well, Sir. It shows." I don't know what it was about him, but he actually made me want to pretend I was cold and snuggle up to him. Even the small talk we exchanged about his vehicle had undercurrents of something dangerous swirling underneath. It was weird and exciting ... and scary.

As he drove out of the library parking lot and onto the street, he said, "I got your tea."

"Thank you! I'm looking forward to it."

Obviously not a man of many words and he subsided into a deep silence after that. Though I tried to start a conversation from time to time, he had reverted back to his hard and tough exterior and all I got were a few grunts and almost unintelligible mutters. He was turning into quite the psychological experiment. Still, I wasn't unhappy with the silence. I sat perfectly still in the seat, listening to the sound of the engine and the world rushing by outside the window.

The drive out to the house didn't take as long as it did when I was with Elaine; perhaps the knot of nervousness in my stomach was not there this time. The winding curves told me he was taking backroads.

He didn't say another word until we pulled into the drive. Then it was simply, "stay right there" as he got out of his side and came around to mine.

By the time he got there, I was standing outside the truck.

"I told you to wait," he said, an edge to his voice.

"If you want me to wait next time, ask politely," I told him.
"And only if you are opening the door because you are a gentleman. Not because I'm blind."

There was a moment of silence. He was obviously taken aback, but his response was very measured. "I have no doubt you are quite capable of getting out of the car yourself. I wasn't opening the door for you because you're blind, but because the ground right now is slick as warm owl shit, and I damn near busted my ass twice this morning."

"Warm owl shit?" I laughed so hard it hurt.

He took my hand as I was still howling and began to lead me to the steps. My feet suddenly went out from under me, and I stopped laughing pretty quick then.

"See?" he said.

Neither of us spoke again until we were in the house. It was way too treacherous to do anything but try to stay upright.

Thirteen

Lara

Once in the house, Kit seemed to be entirely out of his element again. Awkward and oddly shy. "There's no fire. Shall I light one for you?"

I shook my head. "Not on my account."

"There's a wood stove in the kitchen. It'll be warmer. Do you want to sit there?"

"Okay," I agreed easily.

"Follow me then."

"It's lovely and warm in here," I said as we entered his kitchen. It smelled of bacon and beans.

He grunted and pulled out a chair. I went and sat on it. He bustled around the kitchen. I heard the tap running to the left, the sound of a kettle filling. He took three steps, which would be my four steps to the right and I heard him put the kettle on and light the stove. He turned around to face me.

"I've got the water boiling for your tea."

"Thank you." I smiled at him.

His voice was again that gruff, leave-me-alone tone. That was fine. After all, we weren't here to share our deepest and darkest secrets. I was there to read to him, and he was supposed to listen quietly.

I waited as he went back over to the stove, banged a few pots and pans, cursed, set down a piece of silverware in front of me, something else thudded next to it, before he came over and sat a steaming cup or mug on the table.

"Thank you," I said, and reached out for it.

It was a cup with no saucer. I wasn't surprised. There was nothing genteel or any false sophistication about the man. He didn't play the games others did. He set his own rules. The silverware was a teaspoon, and the other thing he put down was a bowl of sugar. Its lip was chipped.

"Milk," he said, and put it next to my cup.

By the full sound of the thud, I guessed the milk was still in its carton. My fingers moved towards it. He had already unscrewed the top for me. I poured what I needed into my tea and followed it with two spoons of sugar.

I stirred my tea and took a sip. "Ahhh ... it's perfect," I sighed, and pushing it to one side, said, "Shall we start?"

Kit placed a book on the table in front of me and I slid my hands across the cover, reading it eagerly. "*Money*," I said. "By Martin Amis." I tasted the name on my tongue again. "Martin Amis. I've never read anything from this author before."

The chair across from me creaked as he sat down in it. Was he going to sit there and watch me as I read? Or was he going to close his eyes and lose himself in the words? I took some time to orient myself to the book, feeling every inch of it. I felt the thrill that always came with a brand-new book, a little happy dance in my heart. Books were fascinating.

"Do you know anything about him?"

He sounded puzzled. "Why?"

"Usually the more I know about the author, the more sense a book makes to me. It's almost as though an author has a certain signature, one that adds a tone to the book that is unique to that author. No matter who they are, they always leave a trace of themselves in their creations."

"Huh ... well, he's British and he's known for having a gift for satire. Black humor. He seems bitter to me. Like an ignored child." His voice was strange, almost challenging me to ask further questions.

"Bitter? Is he, now?" I said, thinking that I had probably just learned more about Kit than about the author.

I opened the book and read the cover pages.

"*Money ... a Suicide Note*?" I tilted my head. How curious.

He chuckled under his breath.

I took a sip of my tea and turned through the first pages. I skimmed over the title pages and got right to the fun part. My fingers found the first words:

> *This is a suicide note. By the time you lay it aside (and you should always read these things slowly, on the lookout for clues or giveaways), John Self will no longer exist.*

Oh, this was going to be interesting indeed!

I read clearly but normally, as if I was just reading to myself. About halfway through the first page I heard a strange sound from Kit. If appreciation could take the form of a snort, that's what I heard.

I stopped.

"You read well," he said gruffly, and there was a reluctant touch of admiration in his voice. He followed that sentence with silence, and I took that as my cue to continue.

I started reading again. It was a book I would never have picked up, not in a million years. To start out, it had all kinds of Britishisms and slang terms that were totally foreign to me, and it was sophisticated in the way I was not.

The narrator was a thirty-five-year old half-British, half-American, jaded film director called John Self who quickly turned out to be a self-loathing, chain smoking, hard drinking, pleasure seeking, pornography loving, sexist pig!

He actually reminded me of the first time a snake was put into my hands. I knew I should be repulsed. I knew it was a cold-blooded poisonous, unfeeling reptile. I was told to expect its skin to be scaly and horrible. Somehow I even got the impression that it would be slimy like an earthworm.

But when I touched the snake, its body was warm and dry, and the scales were a pretty diamond pattern. It made a whispery sound as it swayed along my arm, and there was something quite wonderful about the way its strong muscles ripped underneath its skin. Then its thin tongue came out and flicked at my skin. Ticklish.

John Self was the snake moving up my arm! I was totally fascinated by him. The man was on the fast lane to Disasterville.

By the first few paragraphs he had got himself kicked out of a cab on Ninety-Ninth street on a rainy night because he called a racist New York cab driver a scumbag. Next, he hit a topless bar on Forty-Fourth, drank too much, watched a girl dance like a vicious wet dream, and for his troubles, got kicked out of that joint too.

After the first chapter, I stopped to take a long sip of my tea.

"What do you think of the book?" Kit asked.

"I'm not sure yet," I said with a smile, and returning my fingers to the raised bumps, continued reading.

Very shortly after that I started feeling sorry for John Self. The man was such a hot mess. With every page his situation got worse and worse.

"Jesus, I never meant me any harm. All I wanted was a good time," he cried, in his self-absorbed, baffled way, after he had overindulged in junk food, alcohol, and a stack of dirty mags. He had an English girlfriend, Selena Street, whom he referred to as a "hot bitch", who wore "top dollar underwear", and was "fucking someone else. A lot—all the time."

"I'd better give you the lowdown on Selina—and quick," he confided to the reader, before cheerfully admitting to lecturing her about the intimate connections between rape and her summer wardrobe!

I stopped reading and attuned my senses towards Kit. “Are you a misogynist?”

Fourteen

Lara

"What?" he seemed genuinely shocked. "I ... uh, no. No, I'm not. I respect women."

"Hmm ..."

"Are you seriously trying to equate me with a fictional character?" His tone was not offended, rather it was curious, probing.

"Not really, but it *is* interesting that you chose this particular book."

"Is the subject matter too unpalatable for you?" he countered softly.

I could feel him staring at me intensely. I felt as if there was much riding on that question. That he would have been disappointed if I had said yes. His gaze was like a physical caress on my skin and it made my fingers itch. I was dying to map his face so I could know exactly who I was dealing with.

"The subject matter doesn't bother me," I said finally, taking another sip of tea. It had gone cold.

"Would you like fresh tea?" he asked.

"Why, thank you," I said, surprised that he had noticed.

I heard him stand and go to the kettle. "So what's the problem?"

While he was opening the container with the tea bags in it, I tapped my fingertips restlessly against the table. “It’s just that you obviously knew what this book was about, and I am willing to bet you’ve already read it at least once. And yet you wanted me to read it aloud. What’s that about?”

He fidgeted with something that was lying on the counter near where the kettle was boiling.

“I just wondered what it would be like to hear someone else read it.”

I knew instinctively that he was not telling the whole truth. “Not someone else,” I guessed slowly. “A woman. A female voice reading a book about a man who celebrates being prejudiced against women.”

There was more shifting. He seemed uncomfortable that he had gotten to a point of such scrutiny. “It’s not like that,” he denied.

“What is it like then?” I pressed.

“I am not prejudiced against women,” he shot back. “One of my best battle buddies was a woman. She served with me in the sandbox and damned if she wasn’t the best of the best. She could take heat from anybody and give it right back. I was impressed with her, always will be.”

“You were in the military with her?” I didn’t know why, but I held my breath. Maybe I would always hold my breath when people talked about the military.

“We were in Mosul together.”

A spear pierced my heart, right where the grief had resided for years. Just waiting to remind me of my terrible loss. I could still feel their faces, the warmth of their skin. I turned away from them angrily. It was useless to dwell on the past. They were gone forever, like a river running away from me. No matter how much I wanted them to come back they never would.

I took a deep breath. My voice when it came out was accusing and unnecessarily combative, and I regretted it even before I finished speaking. "Why would someone who claims a woman was one of his best battle buddies enjoy a story about a man who has no use for women as anything but sex objects?"

For a few seconds he didn't reply. I knew he was surprised by the venom in my voice. I nearly apologized.

"To see how the other half lives," he said lightly.

I laughed out loud, relieved that he had deliberately not responded to my rudeness. He didn't join me in my mirth and something told me that I'd gone and hung my saddle on the wrong horse. He was not a misogynist. There was something far more important than John Self's degradation of women that was at play here. My laughter died suddenly and I got serious.

"So, really ... why this book?"

There was a long moment of shuffling from Kit's side of the table. "Because it's about a guy trying to figure out who he is. Trying to make his way through a shitstorm of what's not real to find what is."

"But there are many other books out there about someone trying to find themselves," I pushed. "Why this particular one?"

"Because ... I don't know, okay?"

His defensiveness made me lean back against the chair. "You do know. You just don't want to tell me."

He got up from his chair, suddenly, his chair screeching on the floor, making me jump. He walked away, big angry steps, and came back a moment later to pour fresh, hot tea into my cup. He put the teapot down with a slight thud. Whatever he was feeling it was being tightly controlled. "Why do you care?" he asked. There was a flare of pain in his voice.

I was startled. "Why wouldn't I?"

"Most people around here think I'm a fucking axe murderer and my wife is buried under the floor of my woodshed."

"You know about that?" I blurted out.

"Someone should teach the good folk of Durango Falls how to whisper." There was neither bitterness nor malice in his voice. He didn't care what they thought.

I grinned. "They do speak loud enough to wake the dead, don't they?"

"I'm surprised my poor dead wife hasn't risen up from under the floorboards and gone to haunt them," he said dryly.

I laughed and imagined him smiling, his lips turned up, the smooth scars on his face stretching. We stopped laughing at about the same time. A strained pause followed. I felt the face of my watch. I had already been there for forty minutes.

"Tell me the truth, Kit. Why is this book so important to you? Please. I'd like to know."

I heard him shuffling his boots on the floor. When he spoke his voice was halting, distant, as if he was looking back far into the past. "I knew someone once. He was my half-English buddy. His mother was from England. She didn't want him to enlist. She used to call him all the time and cry like a baby for him and beg him to come back. We all used to leave the room when she called. It was heartbreaking. I don't know how he could bear it. I think she always knew that he wouldn't come back to her."

The hairs on the back of my neck stood. That is exactly how I felt when my brother enlisted and left for Afghanistan. I knew he was not coming back. But just his friend, no matter how much I cried and pleaded with him, he was determined to fight for his country. I clenched my fists tightly to stop the tears that prickled at the backs of my eyes.

"At night he would take this book out of his bag and read it. It was his favorite book. He tried to get me to read it, but I gave up after a few pages. It was not my kind of book. A pussy whipped, self-indulgent sap like John Self was not my idea of a hero."

He made a raw sound in his throat.

"Then Nigel got hit. Friendly fire. Fucking worst two words in the dictionary. You die like a dog on foreign fucking soil for nothing. As he lay white with pain in the truck he bawled for his mother. There was not a single thing any of us could do. We just sat there and watched him bleed out. When they went to tell his mother I heard that she slapped the men who brought the message."

He paused and took a deep breath of regret or pain.

"After a month the book came to me in the post. He had left it to me in his will. I sat down and read it from cover to cover. And I heard the words in his voice. I realized that we are all John Self. Every fucking one of us. Lost in our vices, drinking too much, eating too much, watching too much porn, indulging ourselves."

He sighed heavily. "I guess I wanted you to read it to see if it would still sound the same," he said.

"Does it?"

One of his wolves howled outside. Inside, the air was thick with some strange emotion.

"No," he whispered finally. "You're not tainted like the rest of us."

Before I could say anything further, his voice turned gruff again. "It's almost time for you to go. Let's stop here and I'll drive you home."

Fifteen

Lara

“Cause if you don’t leave this town,
you might not make it out.”

https://www.youtube.com/watch?v=v4pi1LxuDHc

I walked out of the post office excited about the new batch of gold paint in my backpack, dreaming of how I would mix it with that warm color called pink. I thought about how I’d splatter it on the mermaid’s sculpture I was working on, almost certainly on the tail, when I came to a sudden stop.

“Hello Sheriff,” I greeted. Sheriff Bradley had never been anything but polite and solicitous to me, but I didn’t like him. Never had. Probably never would. From the time I was a kid, something about him made my skin crawl. And he knew it too.

“I hear you’re working for Carson now,” he said. He was smoking, and I felt the smoke in my face. Because I couldn’t see he thought I wouldn’t know that he had deliberately blown it in my face.

“Yeah, I’m reading for him twice a week,” I said, waving the smoke from my face.

"He's not doing anything weird or kinky to you, is he?"

I felt so angry I wanted to punch his face. I knew exactly where that smoke hole was too. "No, he's not," I said tightly. "He's actually a gentleman."

"A gentleman?" he sneered.

I heard him widen his stance into a challenging pose. "So why does he need a blind girl to read to him?"

I shrugged casually. "He just doesn't want anyone to see his face."

"Isn't that weird?"

"No, it's not, Sheriff Bradley. It's not. He's a shy, kind man who has scars."

"Does he ever ... touch you, or do you hear him ... er ... touching himself?"

I felt my hands clenching with fury. "No. He has *never* behaved inappropriately with me."

"Good. You will tell me if he tries anything, won't ya? I take care of my flock."

"You'll be the first person I come to if he tries anything, Sheriff," I said. Not. I'd rather cut my right arm off than go running to him.

"I'll be seeing you, then. Good day."

I nodded and waited until he passed me by.

This was the beginning. Soon the whole town would be warning me, and telling me I was making a big mistake. That my very honor was at stake. I walked over to the library still hopping mad. Thank god Elaine was there. I took my knitted cap off.

"Can you believe Sheriff Bradley asked me if Kit was touching me, or himself during our reading session? The man's an ass!" I fumed.

"Oh, Lara. You better get used to it. You know the whole town is going to wonder ... and they're going to make up a ton of stuff about you and him. The best way to deal with it is to give them some details so they can't make stuff up."

I gasped. "Are you serious?"

"Of course. You tell me exactly what's going on and I'll pass it on."

I shook my head in wonder. "Elaine. Nothing is going on. I'm just reading to him."

"Lara. You're going to have to do better than that. Nobody, and I mean nobody, is going to believe that shit. Come on. At least tell me that he tried it on and you slapped him down."

"What? No. He didn't do any such thing."

"Of course he didn't. But it does sound good, doesn't it?"

My jaw dropped. "Elaine Crockett, this time you've gone too far. Kit Carson is a good man, and I don't want you spreading any more lies about him. If I hear anything bad about him, I'll swear I'll never speak to you again," I said, and turning around I began to walk towards the entrance. I was so furious my hands were shaking. Elaine ran after me and grabbed my arm.

"All right. All right. I won't say anything bad about him," she coaxed.

I drew a shaking breath. "Promise?"

"Promise."

"I'm gonna trust you, Elaine, to keep to your word. That man has suffered enough. He's a really nice guy, and I don't want to hurt him any more than he has already been."

"It's not like he's going to know, is it?"

"For your information he already knows all the horrible things the townsfolk have been saying about him."

"How?" she asked, sounding quite startled.

"How do you think?"

"Well, I can't be responsible for people who can't keep their voices down," she said defensively.

"Please, Elaine, I beg of you. Don't start any nasty rumors about him and me. Think of me if you can't think of him."

She grabbed my shoulders and planted a noisy kiss on my cheeks. "I'm sorry, Lara. You know I love you. I just get carried away sometimes. I'll never do anything to hurt you."

I frowned. "What about him?"

She sighed dramatically. "Yes, I won't do anything to hurt him either."

I grasped her hands in mine. "Okay. Thank you."

"Want some oatmeal cookies?" she offered, completely changing the subject.

I hesitated. "Who made them?"

"Ma."

"You just promised not to do anything to hurt me."

She laughed. "Just kidding. Grandma baked them."

"Lead me to them, and be quick about it, will ya?" I said with a grin.

Sixteen

Kit

Some people feel the rain. Others just get wet.
-Bob Marley

I sat in my pickup and stared at her as she crossed the snowy carpark. It was like watching an angel, all blonde and glorious, come towards me. I got out, went around to the passenger side, and held the door open.

"Hello, Mr. Carson," she greeted as she got nearer.

"Miss Young," I said formally, but there was that lilt in my voice that only came when she was around.

Today she had brought a faint but extremely delicious scent with her. I sniffed the air as she climbed into the truck. It was coming from her backpack.

With a song in my heart I went around to my side. Inside the truck the smell intensified. It hit me in the gut the moment I got in, and damn near knocked me flat. My reaction was the equivalent to what you'd see when my wolves catch the scent of warm rabbit. I started salivating. I felt the empty, hungry hole right through my middle. My stomach growled so loudly she had to have heard it.

Her voice was chipper and full of laughter. "I'm glad you're hungry, because I brought cupcakes for us."

No kidding, can I have some, how many are there, can I have more than one, come in, come in! It was a long, long time since vanilla icing melted away in my mouth.

"It sure smells good," was what I actually said. "Thank you."

I lived with the scent of those luscious things all the way back, which I admit made me drive a whole lot faster than I usually would on dangerous roads. I parked as close to the house as I could. Fortunately, there had been a break in the cold spell and getting into the house wasn't as treacherous. Except for Chepi who came for a quick, wary rub. The other wolves hung around at a safe distance. I didn't hold Lara, or anything like that, but I watched her like a hawk as she made it up the path to the house.

As soon as I opened the front door she walked in and made straight for the kitchen. She put her backpack on the kitchen table and pulled out a box of cupcakes from it. I was impressed by how quickly she had learned her way around the house. When she turned back to look at me she pegged where I was right away, as though she could actually see me. Her sense of direction was uncanny.

"Nothing like sweet cupcakes to go along with a bitter book," she said.

I had to grin at that. "I'll put the kettle on."

"Will you have some tea with me?" she asked.

I didn't have it in me to say no and that was how I wound up sitting across the table from an angel in disguise, taking small sips of something that tasted like hot dishwater from a chipped cup (I gave her the good one) while she opened up the box of cupcakes.

It was damn near surreal, that cozy scene right there in my kitchen.

I looked at the cupcakes, at how perfectly iced and decorated they were, and paused. "Did you buy these?"

"No, I made them. I am a fantastic baker," she said, without any false modesty. Reaching into the box she brought out a cupcake for me, then one for herself. "I can't cook worth a damn, but I can bake like nobody's business."

"But that's really ... intensive work, right? Lots of tiny measurements?"

She shrugged. "I like that part of it. I know it seems like it would be hard for me, but it's not. I like a world that can be measured and planned out. I do it to relax. Especially when people annoy me."

I stopped peeling the sparkly paper off the cake. Was that a hint? "Has someone been annoying you?"

"Don't worry it's not you," she said with the biggest grin I had ever seen. I loved her grin. It was so open, trusting and vulnerable. There was nothing behind it. You could trust it.

I watched as she broke her cupcake in half, then turned the top of it upside down. With a naughty smile she pushed the two halves together, squishing the icing in between the two layers. It oozed out one side onto her slim fingers. I watched as she licked it from her skin.

My body suddenly didn't want to behave. I shifted in my seat and I stared at her hungrily. I wanted to fucking eat her, not the cake.

Holding her cupcake like a cheeseburger she leaned forward and, opening her mouth wide, took a generous bite out of the sweet sandwich. When she pulled back, her whole mouth was covered with icing and her eyes were closed with pleasure.

"I am such a fucking *good* baker!" she growled.

The laugh came out of nowhere, bubbling out of me faster than I could control it. Ah, hell, why not? I let it roll out, booming out my chest like thunder far too close. It felt so good that I did it again.

Then Lara took another bite, and with her mouth stuck out her tongue like a child, and damned if it wasn't funny, if I didn't absolutely lose it. I laughed so hard it hurt – my ribs, my chest, my throat, my lips, all of it actually ached. Lara laughing hard seemed to keep me going, too–it was contagious.

In the midst of that surprise pleasure, a strange thought came to me:

How long had it been?

How long had it been since I laughed with another human being? Really, truly laughed? My mind went back through the long years I had spent in that house, and I finally came up with an answer. Never! The last time I had laughed was when I saw the littlest wolf, Benjamin, go after a snowshoe hare, and go tip over top through the snow. He came up with a look of such complete surprise that I had to laugh at the little booger.

That was three months ago.

The silence after the laughter was comfortable. I ate one cupcake the old-fashioned way, and then turned the second one into a sandwich. Lara began to read. Her sweet voice flowing over me as I bit into the cake. The world was good.

I decided I liked the cupcake better the sandwich way.

Seventeen

Kit

Outside it had begun to snow lightly. I could see the wolves milling about in the backyard, and by the grove of trees where they liked to hide out. Inside, it was warm. Through the small square of glass set into the cast iron door of the wood burner, the red-orange glow of the flames spilled out and lit up Lara's face as she sat opposite me.

Her coat was draped around the back of the chair, and she was in a pink and blue floral sweater, with the collar of her red shirt underneath peeking through. There was some kind of yellow scarf tied loosely around her neck and a green hair band on her head.

She should have looked like a human bag of Skittles; instead she resembled a warm scene on a Christmas card. One of those that reminded you of a tree full of glittery decorations, a roaring fire, laughing children, a table heaped with good food, spicy scents in the air, and the sound of exploding crackers.

I feasted my eyes on her, safe in the knowledge that she would never know I was staring, or even begin to imagine how much pleasure I took from watching her smooth skin, the apple like tightness of her rosy cheeks, and the way her plump mouth moved as she read quietly.

I took a sip of my whiskey. Yeah, me and tea decided to part company after our first meeting. She must have heard me, because she stopped and reached for her cup.

"Thank you," I said softly.

"You're welcome!" The teacup remained suspended midair as she smiled. It was genuine, open. Like a child's. "Although, you don't need to thank me. Turns out I'm really enjoying this demonically comic book. John Self as the narrator of his own train wreck is pure genius, and taking money to read this seems almost unfair."

"I meant ... thank you for everything. All of it."

She put her teacup down without drinking from it. "All of it?"

"I guess what I'm trying to say is it's nice to have company."

"You don't like company, Mr. Carson. You mean you like *my* company."

She grinned irrepressibly. *What a sweetheart!* I wanted to touch her. My hand even lifted, then dropped. "Yeah. You ... brighten the place."

She laughed. "You make me sound like an ornament."

I sighed. "Okay, you win. I like your company."

"I'm glad, because you were mighty ornery that first day I was here."

"I know I was rude to you then, and I'm sorry. I've been holed up for so long with no one for company but my wolves. I've forgotten how to act around a lady."

She nodded slowly. “Luckily for you, Mr. Carson,” she said with an exaggerated Southern drawl, “I ain’t no lady. My Ma used to call me a right hooligan.”

I shook my head even though she couldn’t see me. “I have trouble believing that.”

“Do ladies put cow crap into people’s shoes?” she asked impishly.

I laughed. “You did?”

She took a sip of tea. “Afraid so.” A considering expression came into her face. “What’s the baddest thing you ever did?”

An involuntary sound tore out of my throat. The baddest thing? Oh, Jesus! I closed my eyes. My insides were quaking. No, I can’t go there. Not with her. She lives inside a Christmas card.

She frowned anxiously. “I’m sorry. I didn’t mean to pry or make you remember anything painful. I only meant as a child what was the baddest thing you ever did? You don’t have to answer it.” Her hand shook as she put the teacup back on the table. “I’ll just continue reading.”

I couldn’t help it. I couldn’t see her hurt. Without thinking, my hand reached out and covered hers. Two things happened simultaneously. My dick became hard and she froze with shock. I snatched my hand back. My body started throbbing with sexual tension.

I don’t know where the hell it came from but I wanted her so fucking bad it hurt. Her hand stretched out tentatively towards me. I was dying to grab it, sweep her into my arms, and kiss her senseless, but I balled my hands into fists, and forced myself not to. I would only ruin her. She wanted a friend. I wanted to spread her legs and bury my cock in her sweet pussy.

I wanted to make her mine.

"There is nothing for you to be sorry for, Lara," I said. My voice was harsh.

She was too naïve to understand the raw need in my voice. She took it as a rejection. Her hand dropped back to the table, and the color drained out of her cheeks. She looked devastated.

Jesus, in my stupid, bumbling way, I caused that! I felt worse than I would have if I'd kicked a puppy. I hated hurting her. Silently, her hands moved towards the page. They fumbled uncertainly, looking for the last sentence she had read.

"When I was six years old," I began, and her fingers stopped moving on the page. I swallowed and continued. "I did a very terrible thing. Far, far worse than putting cow crap in someone's shoe."

I watched her plump lips tremble and part as she exhaled the breath she was holding. A ghost of a smile appeared, and it made me ridiculously happy to see it.

"My father had gone to the mall and he'd taken my brother and sister with him. I was not allowed to go with him because I had broken my brother's favorite toy. I was furious so I splattered ketchup all over my stomach and chest, fired my father's shotgun out of the window, and let my mother find me on the ground with the gun on top of me, with my eyes wide open as if I was dead."

She gasped with shock.

"That was the baddest thing I ever did as a child."

"What did your Ma do?" she whispered.

"Before or after I blinked and laughed at her?"

"After, I think?"

"She went crazy and then took me to the kitchen and gave me cookies and milk. I got the whopping of my life when my Dad came home, though."

"I'm not surprised. That's unbelievably naughty."

"What else do you want to know about me, Lara?"

She blushed. Oh, but she was beautiful. "I wouldn't know where to start, Mr. Carson. I have so many questions for you."

I was caught completely by surprise by that. "You do?"

"Absolutely. You're quite the mysterious man around town, you know." She smiled.

"I thought I was just a run of the mill, blood drinking, axe murderer," I mocked.

She smiled. "Yes, but there are other things they say about you too."

"Do I want to know?"

"Some of it ... is actually quite fun," she said cheekily.

"Yeah, like what?"

"They say you make your own shine. You have a whole factory in the forest. Barrels and barrels of it."

I laughed at the nonsense the town folk had been making up about me. "Sorry to disappoint, but no. I don't make shine. I don't even know how to."

"Awww ... and I was going to buy a bottle off you."

"Sorry."

"I think I know exactly what I want to ask you!" she blurted out suddenly. Her face was intense, and I braced myself for what was coming.

"What is it?" I asked. I figured she would ask about my military service. About why I stayed out here in the middle of nowhere. About what my life had been like before I came here. She could even ask me how I got my scars, but what she wanted to know took me by surprise.

"Tell me about your wolves," she invited.

Eighteen

Kit

She hit on the one thing I could talk about all day long.

The wolves were my companions, my family, my babies – even though they were wild animals, and I was committed to keeping them that way, but that distance didn't mean I didn't understand them as well as I understood myself. I knew instinctively when they were in trouble. Once I was sitting in the kitchen eating a meal, when I felt my stomach become uneasy. It was so strong I couldn't eat another forkful.

So I went out of the house and stood on the porch. It was summer and the evening was still young. I grabbed my Wolf Pack Howling Horn and began to walk. Every now and again I blew into my horn. It imitated their howls. I walked for an hour until one of my wolves responded to my horn. I found Thomas caught in a thorny hedgerow.

When you help an animal facing down death, it recognizes your deed, and shows its thanks in whatever way it can. Not in the cheesy way we're taught by watching Hollywood movies about animals, but in a subtle way.

In the case of an Alpha like Thomas, he came onto the porch whenever I was there. Even though he kept a space between us most of the time, every now and again he would come to check me out, and give me the gift of petting him for a while. It was the same with Adam, who roamed wherever he wished, but always came back – not because he needed to be with me, but because he wanted to.

I closed the book in front of her. “Come,” I said.

“Where to?”

“There is nothing I can tell you that my wolves will not tell you themselves.”

I waited for her to get into her coat. I could have taken her to the back door, of course, but the wolves only came there when they would rather beg for food than hunt for themselves, and they could be quite aggressive and feral about their food.

The porch was where I really connected with them, mostly because it was their choice to come up there to meet me. The wide wrap-around porch had plenty of room so they never felt trapped. I never approached them. If they wanted some affection, a little backrub, or two, they came and got it. Except for Chepi, of course. She was so tame she sat beside me and licked my head until it was soaked, and sometimes even curled up in my lap for a nap.

It was still snowing when I opened the door. The air was cold and fresh after the warm kitchen. We stood on the porch for a long moment without speaking. I wanted to let the wolves realize that there was no danger. They could come forward.

There were several wolves down by the fencerow. The usual suspects: Caleb, Eyolf, Felan and Gorg. They normally hung out there until they heard the rare vehicle coming down the road, then they vanished like smoke into thin air. You wouldn't see them again until the traveler was well away.

To the left there was a pack of four on the hillside. They were slowly making their way over to the house. Leading was Kurt. He was always the risk taker and the asshole. Lobo a beautiful pure white wolf was next. Behind them two females, Susi and Tasha, moved with lithe grace.

I looked over and saw Lara. Her face was turned towards the hillside. She must have been listening to them, but how could she have heard them? The sound of their footfalls in the snow was always a spooky kind of quiet.

"How many are there?" she whispered.

"In that little pack? Four."

"Should I pet them, or be scared?" she asked with a nervous smile.

I thought about that. "You shouldn't be scared of them, but they are wild creatures not pets, and they should be treated with a certain respect. Treat them well, and they will return the favor. That is the way it has always been with me."

She nodded as the wolves came closer, their noses up in the air, full of adventure and curiosity. I watched her as she stood very still, her sightless eyes hidden behind her glasses. She reached out to touch the snow covered wooden railing. I watched her small white fingers curl around it, dislodging the snow, and how the skin of her knuckles turned bone white as she clenched the wood. She was anxious.

Then she deliberately took a deep breath, unclenched her hand, and relaxed from head to toe. Her ability to control her natural fear tossed me into a quick decision.

"Let me introduce you," I said.

The wolves were obviously interested, so I knew they would make their way up onto the porch. What surprised me was how quickly they chose to do it. Usually they took their time to decide whether something was a good idea, but they were so nosy about Lara, that Kurt already had his paw on the top step. Faster than I had ever seen. He stared at her with his glowing greenish eyes.

"Slowly turn to your left," I said, "and hold out your hand. Let him smell you. His name is Kurt."

Lara did exactly as I instructed. The two girls hung back warily, as I had expected them to, but to my surprise it was not Kurt who took the first step forward. It was Lobo, my beautiful white albino. With his haunches quivering, he stretched out his neck and took a good whiff of her hand. He took another step closer, and I knew Lara had passed his test.

"I wish you could see them ... they are so curious," I said to her.

"I can feel their curiosity," she whispered.

"Stay right here. They will not hurt you, I promise. I'm going to get some treats for them. I'll be right back."

I turned to the door, but right after I stepped through, I turned around to see what the wolves were doing, and Lobo had stepped even closer, and now he had pressed his nose against Lara's hand. There they stood together, not moving, the beautiful woman and that wild white wolf. My pride in my wolves welled up as Lobo took one more step and pressed his muzzle fully against her hand. Lara slowly turned her fingers over, letting Lobo see exactly what she was doing, and rubbed the side of his nose.

Lobo's eyes drifted closed. I stood there and stared. I honestly could not believe what I was seeing. Then he opened his eyes, stepped back and looked from Lara to me.

"Lara," I called.

She didn't turn her head. "Yes."

"The wolf that came to you is called Lobo. He has chosen you to be his special human. Once a wolf chooses a human it will never again treat another human with the same love and affection that it does to the special person it chose."

"Really? He chose me?" Lara asked excitedly.

"Really," I said softly.

"Oh, I can't believe it. Is he like my wolf now?"

I smiled. "Yes. He is like your wolf now."

She laughed with sheer joy.

"Hang on," I said, and went to get the dried treats from the kitchen.

The wolves recognized the scent well before I got back to the door, and by the time I stepped onto the porch they were all scrambling around in the front yard, the pack of four now joined by another six. I handed the treats to Lara and told her to throw them out as hard as she could.

"They love to chase them down, so put some serious muscle into it."

That's how I learned that for a small thing Lara had some serious muscle. She threw those treats so hard she had them babies running for their dinner. They loved it, and judging by the ecstatic smile on her face, so did she.

Me? I loved watching them all, my wolves and my blind reader.

Nineteen

Lara

The day with the wolves opened up a floodgate of sorts. Kit seemed happy to see me, as if he was actually waiting for our sessions together. Our last reading meet turned out to be us talking the entire time, without a single sentence read from the book.

On the surface we had hardly anything in common, but with every sentence we fell deeper and deeper into an oddly intense and close friendship. There was so much about him that drew me, and the more time we spent together, the more I realized just how much I admired and liked him. Tomorrow I would see him again and already I could hardly wait for the sound of his pickup parking outside the library.

With a sigh I placed the apple pie I had made into the hot oven. I closed the door and set the timer. Taking off my oven mitts I hung them in their place. I was about to start cleaning up the mess when the doorbell rang.

Who could it be? It was nearly ten o'clock at night, and most folks around here were fast asleep in their beds by now. Unless it was Elaine on her way back from the bar, I chuckled to myself. I slipped on my dark glasses and walked to the front room with a slight frown. Elaine didn't say anything about going to the bar.

I stood behind the door and called out. "Who's there?"

"It's Sawyer."

My frown deepened. Sawyer Buchanan! What in God's name was he doing here at this time of the night? I opened the door and smelled his aftershave: citrus with a hint of rosemary and something else musky. Like an expensive version of Pledge.

"Hello, Lara." His voice sounded slightly slurred. Was he drunk?

"Hey," I greeted casually. "What are you doing in this part of town?"

"I was passing and I ... er ... saw the lights so I thought I'd pay a little visit. Can I ... um ... come in?"

My eyebrows rose in disbelief at the blatant lie, but I opened the door wider out of sheer curiosity, and he came into my little house. I heard him close the door and rub his hands together.

"It's bitter out there," he said in his toe curling drawl. There was a time I thought I was in love with him. It wasn't completely my fault that I fell for him. He did kinda lead me up the garden path. He would put his hand on the small of my back, or come so close I could feel his warm breath on my neck. When he kissed me on the cheek his lips used to linger so I honestly felt that he liked me too, but I guess I was wrong. He didn't.

I led the way to the living room. “Can I get you a drink? Milk, orange juice, water?”

“You don’t have anything stronger?”

I had a bottle of French wine that I got for my birthday, but I was saving that for a special occasion, maybe when I finished my mermaid, the biggest project I had ever undertaken. She was almost life-size and had already taken three months of my life. “Not really,” I said softly.

“Nah. Don’t bother, then. I’m not really thirsty.”

“Have a seat,” I invited, waving towards the sofa and walking to the armchair opposite.

I heard the sofa depress under his weight.

“So, what can I do for you, Sawyer?”

“There’s talk around town that you’re mixed up with that oddball hick up at Old Man’s Creek.”

I took a deep breath. “He is not an oddball hick,” I said slowly and clearly.

“Heck, Lara. You don’t know what a risk you’re taking going off with him alone to that godforsaken place. Anything could happen to you.”

I felt my temper rising, but I held myself in check. “As you can see nothing has happened to me. I’m perfectly safe. Mr. Carson has been nothing but a gentleman.”

“I don’t like it.”

Wow. Where did that come from? “I beg your pardon.”

He stood up and started pacing the floor. “Don’t go to his house, Lara,” he burst out suddenly. To my shock he marched up to me, grabbed me by my upper arms, and pulled me upright.

"Sawyer!" I squealed, completely taken aback and confused. What on earth was going on?

He let go of me as suddenly as he had grabbed me. "I'm sorry," he apologized, and took a step back. He seemed so agitated I couldn't think straight or understand what was going on. I heard him move away from me as I rubbed my arms where he had grabbed me.

He came back towards me, and though my instinct was to step back, I held my ground.

"Please, Lara," he begged. "I simply can't bear the thought of you going to his house and spending time with him. It makes me sick to my stomach. I worry about you, you know?"

My mouth dropped open with shock. My mind went blank. What the hell was he talking about? I ran my hand through my hair. I took a deep breath.

"Correct me if I'm wrong, but you're engaged to Kayleigh, aren't you?" I asked. I didn't know Kayleigh, but her family owned most of the land around here, and most of the wealth too. Elaine went to school with her. When I asked her to describe Kayleigh, she just snorted, and said in a sour voice, "Just imagine a cow wearing a tiara, then imagine it being snooty to boot." But I knew it wasn't true. Kayleigh was beautiful. There was even talk of her becoming a model.

He made a tortured sound. "Yes, yes, yes, I know goddamnit, but fucking hell, you know that I'm in love with you."

I felt cold all over. "What are you talking about?"

"I loved you from the moment I first laid eyes on you," he declared passionately.

"You didn't want me. I offered myself to you, remember?" I cried.

"Oh, Lara. What a little innocent you are. I love you, I always have, surely you know that, but I can't marry you."

It hit me then and I took a step back. "Because I'm blind?"

"No, no, you little fool. I wouldn't care if you were legless and armless."

"Why then?" I whispered.

"Fuck."

"Tell me," I yelled suddenly.

"It's money, okay? It's her fucking money," he screamed back.

I fell backwards into the chair, breathing hard. "This is crazy."

"I can't bear to lose you to that, that murderer."

"Murderer?" I repeated in a daze.

"Everyone knows he killed his wife."

"He did not murder his wife," I said quietly.

"How do you know that?"

"I just do."

"Yeah, and everybody thought John Gacy was just a clown."

"I don't get it, Sawyer. You're going to marry Kayleigh. What do you want from me?"

"I want you to be my sweetheart, Lara."

A disbelieving laugh escaped my lips. "You want me to be your whore."

"No. It's not like that. I love you."

"Not more than Kayleigh's father's money it would seem," I said bitterly.

"It'll just be a marriage of convenience. It's you in my thoughts, my heart, my soul. I love you, Lara. Please, just wait for me. I swear, we'll be together one day soon. I *want* to marry you. With every fiber of my being." He stopped to take a deep breath. "Just give me two years. That's all I need. I have a plan. Old man Havington has promised me that I'll be head of his business. I'll work hard and make enough money for us. Enough to take care of you. You won't ever have to work again."

"Two years?"

"Yes," he cried eagerly. "Two years is nothing. It'll fly, you'll see. Just please don't give yourself to anyone else until them."

"What if you have kids, Sawyer?"

"I'll let her keep them. I only want the kids we make together."

I shook my head in wonder. "I used to envy Kayleigh. I used to think she had everything, money, looks, you. I used to dream of you, but you know what? I pity her now."

"You don't have to pity her. She knows I don't love her. She just wants to hang on the arm of the best looking man in Durango Falls."

I shook my head sadly. "Then I pity her more. Good luck with your life, Sawyer. I'll certainly not be waiting for you."

He knelt in front of me. I could smell the alcohol on his breath and I hated it. To think I cried for this man. What a silly girl I was.

"Please, Lara. Please. Please understand," he urged desperately.

"I understand perfectly."

"No, you don't. I want to give you everything. Everything I'm doing is for you. Say you'll wait for me. Please don't go to that crazy wolfman."

"You're not half the man he is," I said through clenched teeth.

He jerked forward, and suddenly his lips were on mine. Wet and insistent. For a second I was paralyzed, then I opened my lips and bit down hard. He screamed and fell backwards. "You bit me," he cried incredulously.

"Get out," I said, wiping my mouth. I could taste his blood. "Get out and never come back."

"This is not over. I'm not giving up," he yelled, but he picked himself up and rushed out. I listened to the door slam then began to cry. I had no one.

Everybody who really loved me was gone forever.

Twenty

Kit

https://www.youtube.com/watch?v=wutmEjdbedE

I opened my eyes to pale blue light stealing into the room. The fire had gone out hours ago, and the tip of my nose was numb with cold. My first thought was, *She won't be coming today.*

I sighed, and my breath turned into white smoke. The days when she was not due to come over had started to stretch like endless wastelands that I had to trudge across. I shut my eyes and thought of her in her home fast asleep, and felt a strange sense of peace.

I imagined her sightless eyes closed. Would she be dreaming now? How did people who had never had sight dream? I decided to ask her the next time I saw her. She was full of surprises. The other day she surprised me by saying she "watched" movies.

The thought of a blind person sitting in front of a screen filled with moving images, and trying to 'get' a movie purely by listening to the sounds coming from it was sort of outlandish. I would have thought nobody would since so much of the stories are told through images, little nuances of hand movements and facial expressions.

But Lara assured me that she did "watch" movies. The last two were The Hunger Games and The Twilight Series.

"What did you think of them?" I asked curiously.

"Well, the music scores were really good, the heroines kicked ass, but the heroes were complete wimps."

That sure made me smile.

"My rating: 3 stars for Twilight and 4.5 for Hunger Games," she said.

"When was the last movie you watched?" I asked.

"Two weeks ago."

"What was it?"

"Spiderman."

"What did you think of it?"

"I thought I was playing it on the wrong speed, or I was watching a rerun of Friends. Not only was it so slow moving, I only managed to squeeze one laugh out of it."

I laughed. "I take it you don't like Friends."

"I think that is one of those programs better left to the sighted," she chirped.

After she left I looked for a DVD I hadn't watched yet, and put it into my player. *Inception.* I closed my eyes and tried to follow the story. Wow! I sure picked a bad movie to start with. I couldn't follow a thing. The temptation to open my eyes was so great I ended up blindfolding myself.

As the movie went on I realized the music was incredible, and created an awesome background, but all the action scenes without pictures were just long unintelligible passages full of gunfire, screaming, grunts, and screeching cars. In the end though, it was all explained and I kinda got it, but it made me appreciate Lara's world a whole lot more.

Instead of taking off the blindfold I walked around my house for a bit. After all, I knew the inside of my house like I knew the back of my hand. Fuck, was that a disaster or what? That night I learned I knew shit about the inside of my house. I banged my knee twice, nearly fell over a chair, and hurt my shoulder on the doorframe when I turned too fast to close the kitchen cabinet. I desperately wanted to take the blindfold off, but I didn't.

This was Lara's world.

It made me appreciate the bravery of blind people. The level of trust they place in each step. When I finally took off my blindfold I went to sit on the porch. It was freezing cold and snow on the ground glittered like diamond dust. The pleasure I got from the wolves and the night was still there, but I missed her. I thought my life would stay on the same path, but ever since she came into my life nothing has been the same.

She was like a tornado, ripping up stuff that I thought was solid and cemented down forever, but damn if that slip of a girl didn't turn my life into something beautiful. Full of life, laughter, joy, cake ... and flowers. Yeah, flowers. Who'd have thought? Me and flowers!

She brought flowers with her the other day.

"I can't see them, but I can smell them," she said. "Besides, you can see them so you might as well enjoy them."

I must have looked a right fool when I went into the grocery store and walked out clutching a bunch of flowers. I don't know where she got hers from, but the ones that I got didn't smell too good. I was a bit embarrassed about it, so I filled an old empty tin with water, stuck them in it, and thought it would be the end of that sorry story, but every time they caught my eye, they reminded me of sweet Lara.

That was Saturday night. Today was Monday. I pulled the blankets up around my neck. Well, she was not coming in today. Which was probably just as well, since I had a bunch of stuff to do.

I needed to get more wood chopped up. Since Lara came into my life I found myself using more wood to keep the place warmer. I don't know why I kept the place so cold and inhospitable. I'd better sort the downstairs window out too. One of the frames was loose and there was talk of a big blizzard rolling in late tomorrow night. One really strong gust of wind and it could blow right off.

The blizzard would probably maroon me in for a couple of days, and the pipes will probably freeze again so I really should fill the bathtub with water, and get enough provisions in for the next couple of days.

I glanced at the alarm clock. It was not yet six. Just enough time to do a bit of hiking up the mountain before the sun came up. Been a couple of weeks since I went up. It was always beautiful at this time of the year. The thought cheered me up, so I pushed away the blankets and walked into a new day.

Only Chepi was around when I came down to the porch. I gave her a piece of bacon and she wolfed it down as quickly as she could. I crouched down and rubbed her gently behind her ear, while she licked my face and made a purring sound.

The air was crisp and sharp. She followed me part of the way, but once I crossed the small frozen lake, she whirled around and went back. I climbed steadily for half an hour while I followed the tracks of a chase. At least five wolves and their prey.

At a clearing I saw the old buck the wolves had pulled down. He had made his last stand with his back to the trees. Poor bastard must have been exhausted from the long winter and the wolves would have been ferocious with hunger. He wouldn't have lasted long. His carcass bore the marks of his predators' attack.

They had bitten into his hamstrings, slicing right through to make it impossible for him to run. His throat was mangled, a crimson river flowed away from his neck, and his eyes were glassy, but there was something valiant about him. He had died fighting an age old enemy.

The wolves had only eaten his entrails, but they would return to their kill later. It was man's traps and poisons that made wolves not go back to finish their meal. There was deep satisfaction in knowing that on my land the wolves had learned to trust again. Here they could roam, hunt, go away and come back to feed without fear.

Wilderness was in balance. The way it should be.

It was a gruesome sight, but the truth was neither wolf nor deer can survive without the other. The deer if allowed to breed unchecked, would overgraze the land and die of starvation, and the wolves without the deer would perish in the winter when the heavy snows hid the small rodents, fish, snakes, grubs, birds, and berries that give them sustenance during the other seasons.

I made my way back down the mountain before the sun filtered through the trees.

Twenty-one

Lara

When the blizzard came, it was on us so suddenly it caught even Kit by surprise. I was sitting at the kitchen table, half-way through chapter twenty-three, when a blast of wind blew hard against the door.

It was so violent I stopped mid-sentence. Kit's chair scraped back abruptly. He walked to the window and said, "Holy smokes."

"Kit?" I called anxiously.

"Damn, it looks like a serious blizzard out there."

"Really?"

"Fuck," he cursed. "The storm got here faster than the weatherman said it would. It was not supposed to arrive till late this evening. Damn, I should have paid better attention to the wolves. Things are always going to get bad when they all huddle up on the porch."

I stood up and reached for my coat. "I should go home before the roads get too bad, then."

"We can give it a shot," Kit said doubtfully. "But it might not be possible. Once we're out of the protection of the windbreak from the trees the storm, if it gets worse, could easily knock my old truck off the road."

"God," I exclaimed alarmed. "How long do you think the blizzard will last?"

"It's not forecast to last more than a few hours, but you can never say. It could even last days."

"Days?" I gasped.

"It's unlikely, but I have to warn you of the worst case scenario. Do you have a pet that needs feeding, or something urgent that you have to do?"

I shook my head.

"Good. We'll just wait and see what happens."

"Wait? For how long?"

"A few hours."

I worried my lower lip. "Are you sure I wouldn't be intruding?"

"No way," he said with a laugh. "I like having you here, remember?"

Outside the wind howled. "What if it lasts longer than a few hours?"

There was an odd silence. "You can sleep in my bedroom. I'll change the sheets for you, and I'll sleep downstairs and make sure the fire doesn't go out."

"I'm sorry to put you to all this trouble," I murmured.

"I never have visitors so it'll be a pleasure," he replied gruffly.

A blast of wind rattled the windows, and I was suddenly excited. I had a brilliant idea.

"Kit?"

"Yeah?"

"Will you do something for me?"

"You want to go home?" he asked, and he sounded so disappointed, I felt bad for him.

I shook my head vigorously. "I want you to be my eyes. I've never been out of town during a blizzard, and I'd love to see it through your eyes."

"Huh?"

"You'll figure something out. I trust you completely."

Kit obviously wasn't sure about my idea, but I was. I wanted to be out there in the midst of the whirling storm.

"Right, get your coat and let's go out onto the porch."

After I slipped into my coat, he came up to me and gave me a warm scarf. It smelled of him and my stomach clenched like a fist. I wrapped it around my neck, and he handed me a pair of thick men's gloves. I pulled them on and he opened the front door. A strong gust of wind carrying fluffy flakes of snow slapped me in the face. I gasped and laughed at the sensation, and felt him turn to stare at me.

"Tell me what you see," I urged.

"It's ... it's cold out here." He stopped. "Obviously, you can feel that yourself," he said, sounding embarrassed. "The wind is blowing hard ... uh ... sorry. Let me start again."

I smiled at him encouragingly.

He was silent while he looked around. "The wolves are milling around out front. They're looking towards us, but none of them have come close yet. When they stand in the snow is when they look most beautiful."

"Come on," he said taking my hand. We went down the steps and stood on the ground. The strong winds full of fluffy snow buffeted us, and tore at my coat, making it flap.

"You know how long the driveway is, right?" he shouted above the noise of the wind.

I turned towards his voice and nodded.

"Okay, on either side of the driveway are sapling trees."

"Cedars," I yelled, my smile widening. "Even in the winter I can smell them."

"That's right," he approved. "They are almost bent over with the strong wind. That roar you hear is the wind tearing through all the big cedars lining the road. But they are good and sturdy, nothing will hurt them."

As the snow poured down on us, Kit called out, "Right now, the blizzard has suddenly got so bad, the air is almost white and you can't see squat. I can't even see the tall cedars out at the road anymore."

Twenty-two

Lara

An hour later we were breaking bread, so to speak.

"I thought you said you couldn't cook?" Kit said from across me at the kitchen table. "This is delicious."

It actually wasn't bad, and I was proud of myself. I had baked the chicken breasts that Kit found in the freezer, and served it along with broccoli and potato salad. Though I had to ask Kit for help in the kitchen, I did most of the work on my own.

I could feel him watching me the whole time, as if what I was doing was nothing short of astounding. Okay, I might have exaggerated my skill, a bit, but it was nice that he was impressed by me.

Kit was not much of a talker, but I was happy for us to eat with only the fury of the wind howling outside.

Finally, Kit pushed his plate away, and sighed with satisfaction. "That was really good. I don't remember the last time I was this stuffed."

I grinned happily. "Good! I'm glad you enjoyed it."

I finished my last bite and pushed my plate away, too.

"I'll wash up," he said, getting up.

"I'll help."

I brought the plates to the sink. He washed and I dried in companionable silence. We worked well together. It was domesticated and cozy. When the last spoon had been dried, and put away, I turned towards him. "Want me to read some more? We're almost done with the book."

"No, why don't we have coffee in the living room? It'll be more comfortable, and you can curl up on the couch with a blanket."

I followed him into the living room where the howl of the wind against the windows was more pronounced. I curled up on one side of the couch as Kit knelt at the fireplace and stoked the flames. When he was done he walked across the room and returned with a thick, soft blanket. He pressed it into my hands.

"I'll go make the coffee. You bundle up," he said. "The house doesn't have much in the way of insulation, so it gets pretty damn cold even with the fire."

I sat listening to the fire crackle and the wolves moving around outside on the porch. It sounded as though there were dozens of them out there, gathering close to each other for warmth. They were hunkering down, much like we were, to ride out the storm.

Kit came in with the coffee, his footsteps muted. I curled my hands around the hot mug and took a sip. It was done just right with two sugars. He settled himself into the armchair opposite me and we drank our coffee together. The warmth of the fire had relaxed him, making him more talkative. He told me about his mother and how he hadn't been home for close to a decade.

"Why?"

"Because I can't be the hero she wants me to be."

"What do you mean?" I asked, surprised.

He made a soft sound of regret. "She was so proud when I enlisted. She told all the neighbors and put up a flag outside the house. She thought I'd be going home decorated with medals. It didn't happen that way. PTSD is not a medal she can boast about in her garden club."

"I think you're wrong. I think your mother loves you no matter what and wants you back."

"You don't know my mother, then. At least, if I don't go back she can still pretend to her friends that I'm some sort of hero. No one but her will know about her misfortune of having the kind of son I have turned out to be."

"I think she is so lucky. You are still alive. So what if you didn't win any medals?" I cried passionately. "I would give anything to have my father and brother back. I wouldn't care if they wore medals, or were suffering from PTSD. I just want them back. No matter what."

Kit's voice was quiet. "What happened to them?"

That old ping of pain was back, right in the center of my chest. I pulled the blanket closer around me, feeling suddenly cold, despite the roaring fire. "My father was killed by an IED in Afghanistan." My voice sounded husky. "And my brother was shot in Iraq. At first they thought he would make it. They even flew him back, but he died in the hospital."

Kit drew a deep breath and slowly exhaled. "I didn't know," he said. "I'm sorry."

"In a way, losing my brother was even harder. My Ma and I went from terror to hope and then to complete loss. He was so young. It was not right. Nobody should die that young." A shiver went through me. "He had so many dreams. For a long time, I hated the Military and I couldn't even bear to be in the same room as a soldier."

I stopped and blinked back the tears.

"And now?" he asked, his voice filled with some unknown emotion.

"Now I've come to terms with it a little. I know Pa and Brad made that choice willingly. They were proud to serve their country. Just like they made their choice, I've made my decision too. I will *never ever* become involved with someone in the military."

He made a strange sound in his throat.

"Don't get me wrong, I don't mind if he *had* been in the military. I just can't do active military duty," I added, and felt my neck and cheeks becoming hot. I hoped I wasn't being too obvious that as far as I was concerned he wasn't on my NEVER EVER list.

I rushed on with more words. "It's just that being married to a soldier takes a certain strength that I do not possess. I would spend my whole life terrified of losing him. I know what my mother went through. Losing her men broke her. After that she was never the same. Even when she was diagnosed with cancer she wasn't interested in healing herself. She went for one round of chemo then she just gave up. Before she died she apologized to me. She said she knew she was being a terrible mother to me, but she just couldn't go on anymore. So you see the army took my whole family away from me."

There was a long silence before Kit spoke again.

"Have you got no other family?" he asked.

"My grandparents from my mother's side are still alive. They moved to Florida when I was a small child, but we're not close. They just send me a present for Christmas, usually books."

"I respect your decision, but just to play devil's advocate. Not having someone you love in the army is not a guarantee that you won't lose him. You could lose him in any way. A car crash. A plane goes down. Even a slip and fall at home that happens at just the wrong angle. That's what happened to my grandfather."

"Oh, I'm sorry, Kit."

Kit cleared his throat. "I was just a baby. I didn't know him. He tripped on something in the barn and hit his head hard on the corner of the old plow. And that was it ..."

I nodded. "I know my view doesn't seem logical to you, but hurt is not logical. My view isn't logical at all, but to my heart, it's the only thing that makes sense."

There was a long moment of silence.

"You must understand. You lost that woman friend you were so impressed with."

"Yeah, I understand. Sometimes things happen that make no sense at all." His voice was suddenly low and sad. He shuffled his feet. The couch moved a bit as he shifted around to his side. Outside, the wind dropped to a low moan. A branch scratched incessantly at the window. Inside, it was warm, safe, and intimate.

"What was her name?" I asked.

Twenty-three

Lara

https://www.youtube.com/watch?v=bqIxCtEveG8

"Valerie. Valerie Pearlman."

"Tell me about her," I asked softly.

"There are a lot of guys who claim they're cool with women in the military, but when it comes down to brass tacks, they really aren't. They can't help feeling that somehow they're going to have to cover or compensate for her. After all, there's no escaping from the fact that women are physically weaker than men."

Kit snorted. "Well, they never met Valerie Pearlman. Damn if that woman didn't run circles around all of us. She was tougher than tough. She showed every one of us! Whatever biases I might have had vanished after my first tour with her. She was, well, she was just something else. I don't know whether it was because she was the bravest person I ever met or the most foolish, by the end of the tour she had become my strongest ally."

"What happened to her?"

"Valerie was killed by an insurgent during a mission in Mosul," he said quietly.

I sucked in my breath. Another life snatched away too soon.

"Three of my buddies were killed that day, but Valerie ... she was the only one who chose to die."

I heard him sigh.

"We should never have been there. We were sent out because of wrong intel. There was nothing in the building. I knew it was a trap even before we stepped out into that compound, but there was no other way out. We were already halfway across when the grenade fucking landed right in the middle of our group. We started to scatter, but my boot got caught on something sticking out of the ground. I went down. Valerie turned around, looked at me and ..." Kit took a long breath. "She threw herself on the grenade."

"Oh, my God!" I whispered.

"It was so simple, Lara. I tripped. That was all. A piece of something on the road, maybe just a tree root, and I fell. Because of that Valerie died." He let out a bitter laugh. "Somebody once said life is a series of accidents so is death."

"Oh, Kit, I am so sorry," I said quietly.

The past became alive in that room. I could tell he was barely holding himself in control. I wasn't helping him much, because tears were running down my cheeks.

Kit stood up and paced around the room. "Wow, we got into some heavy shit here, huh?"

I didn't know how to respond, so I said the first thing that came to mind. "Can I see you?"

Kit paused in his pacing.

I held out my hands. "Can I ... can I feel your face? I have always wondered what you look like."

"Why now?"

"I'd like to see the face of the man I will be spending the night with."

For a long moment he stood frozen, then he spoke, "Valerie saved my life by taking the brunt of the blast, but not all of it. I have horrible scars, Lara." He sounded wary and distant, as if he expected me to shrink away from wanting to feel his face.

"Don't we all? Yours are just more visible than most," I said quietly.

"You sound like a shrink."

I didn't say anything and dropped my head, embarrassed that I had asked him for something so personal. I had never done something so bold before.

Then I heard his footsteps come towards me. Quiet, but determined. He knelt on the floor in front of the couch. "I'll let you see my scars if you let me see your eyes."

I took my glasses off and held them in my lap.

"There's nothing wrong with your eyes. Why do you hide them?" His voice was warm and deep.

"My father bought them for me. I think he was afraid someone would say something hurtful about my eyes."

"Hurtful?" He sounded surprised. "They are different," he paused. "But they're not unattractive. They're you and so they are as beautiful as milky blue marbles. When you are with me, I would prefer if you did not wear your glasses again."

I nodded speechlessly. No one had ever told me my eyes were beautiful. Not even Ma, and I know, no one loved me more than she did.

His hands were warm as they closed over my fingers. Slowly, he lifted my hands to his face, to his forehead. The skin on his face was even warmer than his hands, as if he was flushed with heat.

Gently, I ran my fingertips over his hot skin. His forehead was broad. Straight, silky hair fell over it. His eyebrows were thick and lush His nose was strong and high. It may have been broken once. His eyelashes were surprisingly stubby and craggy. His cheeks were raspy with shadow. In contrast, his lips were surprisingly soft and full, especially the bottom lip, and his scars: I found them on the left side of his face. From the outer corner of his eye right down to his chin. They were smooth and raised, etchings of pain and suffering. I found myself fascinated by them as I lightly traced them with one finger.

At first Kit flinched as I touched them, but I cupped his face in my hands. "The scars suit you. A man living by himself at the edge of a mountain should have such a face," I said. "It's like your story is written on your face in a language only you can understand."

There was a long moment of silence as he contemplated that.

"You make them sound almost beautiful."

"They are not beautiful. You are."

Under my hands, his jaw clenched. Then his hands came up to rest on mine. "Thank you, but that's not true. I am a scarred and unattractive man. I make little children stare," he said.

I shook my head. "No. You're wrong."

Something feral and primitive began to throb between us and I don't know what possessed me, but I leaned forward and pressed my lips against his.

Kit drew in a sharp breath and jerked back. In that split second, I realized I might have misjudged the emotion between us. Perhaps I had made a terrible, terrible mistake. Heat rushed into my face as I opened my mouth to apologize, but the air around me moved, and Kit's lips swooped down on mine. He wrapped his big hands around my shoulders and pulled me in.

He was so careful at first, so hesitant, as if he was afraid he could break me. The stubble on his face pressed against my chin, reminding me of just how virile he was. I suddenly wanted to touch all of him, not just his face. I slid my hand down his chest and that's all it took for him to lose the tight control he was exercising.

His tongue swept into my mouth ruthlessly, demanding and eager, stealing my breath away. His hands slid up to my hair. He wrapped his fingers into it and pulled gently, then harder, tipping my head back for better access to kiss me just how he wanted. The more eager he became, the more I gave it right back to him, until we were both on the couch, lying against each other, kissing so deeply that it was impossible to tell where one ended and the other began.

Kit ground against me once, then twice. I felt his shaft, hard and hot through our clothes. Then

I heard his breath catch in his chest. My heart was pounding so hard I could feel it all through my body, especially right there in my center, right where I was melting from the inside out.

Suddenly he pulled himself away from me.

His absence left me cold, both literally and figuratively. I sat up and reached for him but he gently caught my arms and lowered them to my lap.

"We can't," he said harshly.

"Why?" I asked, my voice unrecognizable with confusion and lust.

"You'll just have to take my word for it that I can't," he muttered.

I heard the steely control in his voice. Then he rose and strode away, his footsteps loud and fast, as if he was running away from me. He stopped at the door.

"I'll go and make your bed."

Then he was gone. I heard him take the stairs two or three at a time while I sat there, dumbfounded.

What the hell just happened?

Twenty-four

Kit

https://www.youtube.com/watch?v=-7XwK2ytJFQ

I still couldn't believe it.

One minute we were just talking, and the next minute she was touching my face, then in the blink of an eye, we were kissing so hard it was like we were devouring each other.

Hell, I almost lost my head.

I was so wild for her I had to force myself to walk away before I threw her down on the floor, ripped her clothes off, and did all the things that I had been dreaming of doing since the first day I saw her.

Even though my balls ached for her sweet pussy, I was glad I walked away. It was one of the hardest things I've ever done, but for once in my brutal life I did the right thing. I saw a delicate little flower and did not crush it under my boot. I was no good for her. She was a sweet, innocent little thing and as surely I was sitting alone in my sleeping bag, I would end up hurting her. Breaking her innocent heart.

I stared into the fire and watched the glowing embers. I was not used to sleeping next to so much heat, but I wanted to keep the house warm for her. I had an image of her asleep in my bed. Immediately, the desire to go up to her pulsated in my loins. I had to stop thinking of her. The blizzard had stopped about an hour ago. Maybe I should go out and spend some time with the wolves. The cold will be good to cool down my heated blood.

I took a few deep breaths. In. Out. Just breathe.

Right when I thought I had things under control I heard a sound on the stairs. I stood up and froze. It was her. She was coming down the stairs. Another couple of creaks and she was standing at the doorway. She was so fucking still; she was like a statue.

My eyes roamed her body greedily. She was so beautiful framed by the velvet darkness behind her. Her honey colored hair was loose down her back and it shone like burnished gold in the firelight. In the flickering light her face was that of an angel. Her feet were bare. My dick became rock hard. I wanted her with every fiber in my body. Every living cell in my body called out for the taste of her flesh.

"Tell me why we can't?" she asked softly.

I didn't move or speak, not that I could have, even if I wanted to. She caught the sound of my breathing and walked toward me. She didn't have her cane, so she moved cautiously, one hand raised in front of her and testing the floor with every step she took. She kept going until her hand collided with my chest. She reached forward, sliding those clever hands up my arms, to my shoulders, until she cupped my face in her fingertips.

"I just want to know why we can't," she insisted.

I caught her hands in mine and swallowed hard. "I don't want to do anything that you might regret, or that might end the friendship we have. It's really good our … friendship, isn't it?"

Her soft lips parted in a silent gasp. "Yes, but I want more."

"Lara, honey."

"I like the way you say my name," she purred. "It sounds almost exotic. I don't know how you do that, but you do."

I cleared my throat and gently took a step back.

"Lara …"

"See? Just like that. You did it again."

She was so small I could crush her with my bare hands. "You know … we could ruin everything. And this is so damn good, isn't it? I haven't had a friendship like this in a very long time."

"How long has it been since you had a lover?"

I choked on my own saliva. My body surged so hard my dick hurt. All I wanted to do was fuck her and I had to give her these bullshit excuses. My heart began a crazy beat. I could feel my blood crashing in my ears. "A really fucking long time," I muttered.

"How long?" she pressed softly.

There was a distant memory, so distant it was goddamn sad. A woman who mattered for a weekend. It was on a beach. A prostitute, but kind. She looked at my dick, and kissed me on the lips to show me that I was not repulsive to her. "You've got the biggest cock I've ever seen, and I've seen a lot, soldier," she said. When she was leaving she told me to call her if I ever needed relief again, but I never did. While I was emptying my cock inside her throat, I was back in Mosul. The white light was exploding all around me, and Valerie was lying in bloody pieces.

"Over a year," I whispered. "Closer to two."

"Huh ... that's not what I expected at all," she said with a smile. "You are so darn sexy I don't know how any woman is expected to keep her hands off you."

Oh, Lara, Lara, my doll. Look at you, saying all the right things. My whole body felt like it was on fire. "Are you actually trying to seduce me? Me? The guy with the fucking burnt face. If you are it's fucking working."

When she stepped forward again and pressed her hands on my shoulders, I had a tough time even thinking about anything else but the gorgeous body that lay underneath her clothes.

"Lara ... are you fucking sure about this?" I whispered hoarsely.

Her answer was to press herself against me as fully as she could. I let her delectable weight push into me. Then I lowered us onto the sleeping bag. To my surprise she climbed right on top of me with no shyness or hesitation at all.

Sinking her hands into my hair she held my face as her lips and tongue worked magic over my mouth, then slowly moved, dropping butterfly kisses all down my chin. By the time she kissed my neck, I knew I was at the point of no return.

"This is your last warning," I said. "Go any lower and I'm gonna be inside you all fucking night."

"Promise?"

Her giggle was that of a carefree child that didn't know better. It frightened the shit out of me. I pulled back, but she grabbed the front of my shirt and pulled me closer, closer, closer.

"I've offered my body to you, please don't say no," she said in a quiet voice.

She obviously had no doubts whatsoever, and suddenly, neither did I. Fuck, it wouldn't be crushing a flower under my boot. It would be more like taking it out by its roots and planting it on my soil so that it would be mine forever. I wrapped my arms around her and rolled us both over onto the sleeping bag, pushing up with my legs until we were both stretched out on it properly. Her head was on my pillow as I hovered above her, and I swear I had never seen anything more beautiful, more innocent, or more delicious than her. I was shaking with the desire.

"You're mine, goddammit," I growled like a fucking Neanderthal.

"Yes," she growled back fiercely. She was like no woman I knew. She cared nothing for niceties.

Then her hands were everywhere. I had rarely been with anyone so eager and it pleased me. I liked it that the little pussycat was a tigress in the sack. I kissed her until she was panting with need. That was what was so unusual and refreshing about her. She didn't pretend to be cool or sophisticated. She made love in the same way she ate cupcakes. With complete abandon. Enjoying every second of it.

I hadn't removed a single stitch of clothing yet, but that was definitely next on my agenda as she arched her back and pulled restlessly at the hem of her sweater. With a few simple movements it was off, and I was staring at a pair of luscious, full breasts encased in a whisper of lace.

I ran my lips up the curve of her breast. Her perfume was stronger here, and I let my tongue explore, hoping to find the tangy spot where she had sprayed it. She gasped as I made my way down her stomach, then back up again, teasing her.

"Take your shirt off," she demanded. "I want to feel your skin."

Twenty-five

Kit

I sat up and did exactly as she asked. When I lowered myself back down on top of her, she wrapped her arms around me and pulled me down so tightly against her that my weight pressed her into the floor.

"You won't be able to breathe," I warned.

"Just stay here a minute," she whispered, her eyes closed and her lips open in pleasure. I kissed her lips again, unable to resist the fullness of them, and she held me there as long as she could before taking a deep, gasping breath. "You feel so damn good."

I slipped my fingertip underneath the lace of her bra. The nipple hiding under there was hard and full. I touched it gently and she arched into my hair, looking for more. "Do you always wear bras this sexy?"

"The panties match," she said with a wicked grin. "You really should look."

"Oh, you think so?" I marveled at how eager she was. She had absolutely no inhibitions about her body. Even the most beautiful women I had been with had hang ups about something and required lots of reassurance that I found them attractive. Lara had none! She didn't know how to compare.

I unbuttoned her jeans and pulled the zipper down slowly, teasing both of us with the reveal. Sure enough, the panties matched.

"Were you looking to get lucky?" I asked, taking my lips on an adventurous trail down her belly to the top of those panties.

"Actually, I always wear things like this," she admitted. "I like all the different textures."

I licked along the top of the panties, right where they met her skin. She gasped and clenched my hair with her hands. I pulled her jeans down more, and she wiggled her hips until they were down her legs. When I finally got them off, she wrapped those long, smooth legs around my shoulders.

It was all the invitation I needed.

I kissed and licked my way up her thighs. She writhed underneath me, her anticipation of what was coming evident in the completely soaked crotch of her panties. I pushed my hand against it, and the moan that came from her was enough to make my cock pulse.

Almost breathless with excitement, I pulled the material to one side – I needed to see all of her – and looked at her pussy. Fuck me. I couldn't take my eyes of it. So fucking pink and sweet, and cushioned under soft panties that clung so lovingly to her gorgeous ass.

The whole thing was like a work of art that belonged in a goddamn art museum, or a shrine. One of those places where people reached on their hands and knees, but an uncivilized heathen like me, I stuck my watering mouth right where it was dripping.

She groaned at the first stroke of my tongue along the dewy puffy folds. Her pretty little pussy was as soft as the petals of a flower and as sweet as holy nectar. My tongue delved deeper as I ate greedily. Her smell intoxicated me and I couldn't get enough.

My hungry slurping drew even louder moans from her as I hit on the spots she loved the most. She pushed her fingers through my hair and arched her hips up to me, giving me more access.

I began drawing designs all over her with my tongue. When I hit a spot that made her shiver and go tense with pleasure, I held her tighter to my mouth and kept at it, rubbing, licking, sucking, worshiping until I found a rhythm that made her moan with ecstasy and her body squirm like a small eel.

"Don't you dare stop," she snarled, driven purely by pleasure.

Don't worry sweetheart. I ain't stopping for nothing. I sucked the engorged button, hard. It took less than a minute before her body became a hard bow. She pushed her clit even deeper into my mouth, and let out a long wail that bounced off the walls. She collapsed underneath me, limp, and completely sated ... not for long. Her little cunt throbbed under my tongue with the power of her orgasm.

"Doggone it, that felt so good!" she said with a shout of laughter.

Sticky-sweet honey was all around my mouth and I licked it clean before I lay down beside her. I rubbed my palm on her nipple over the lace of her bra. It was as hard as a stone. It didn't take long for her to catch her breath and rise up on her elbow.

She grinned at me. "Now it's your turn."

Her searching hands found the button of my jeans and slid the zip down. She fumbled a bit so I helped her push my denims off. As soon as they got to my ankles I kicked them haphazardly away.

Now there was nothing between us but a pair of old boxers. I lifted my hips and she hooked her fingers into the waistband and pulled the thin material down, and my dick jumped to full attention before her. It was throbbing so much to get inside her silky warmth it actually hurt.

Patience, Kit, patience.

Moving on her hands and knees, she climbed up to my thighs and sat nude and upright on them, her wet open pussy rubbing on my flesh. In the firelight she was glorious. She slid her hands up my thighs. They were smooth and delicious on my skin. One hand stumbled upon my upright cock then immediately curled around it. We gasped in unison. Me with the sudden thrill of her soft hand fisting my cock, and her with the shock at my size.

"You're so huge," she whispered in wonder.

"Yeah," I smirked. I knew I was big. I'd been told often enough.

Her hands ran lightly along the shaft and over the pulsing veins. My cock jerked at her touch. Her hand was cool and sure as she slowly slid her fingers up, feeling every inch of me with her sculptor's hands. It was as though she was memorizing me, testing the texture of my skin, exploring me in a way that no other woman had.

"Your skin is like satin, but he seems angry. Is he?" she asked, her face filled with curiosity and tilted to one side.

"No, sweetheart. He's not angry. He's just too fucking excited at the thought of filling every inch of your wet pussy."

She blushed prettily. "He reminds me of a wild bull."

"That's right. He's just waiting for the gates to open so he can ride on in."

"Will all of him fit inside me?" she asked in a voice filled with wonder.

"We'll take it slow," I reassured.

"Don't worry. I'm not afraid at all. I want all of him inside me."

"Good, because I am dying to be inside you."

"Can I taste you first?" she asked.

I wanted to say something, but I swear, I had gone and lost the power of speech.

Twenty-six

Kit

I watched, mesmerized, as she tossed her shining curls back over her shoulder, and almost in slow motion lowered her mouth toward me, torturing me with the wait. Slowly, she moved her hand up and down in sensuously caressing strokes, while her breath blew gently over the head of my cock.

As I watched, she opened her mouth and fitted it over the head of my cock. I clenched the cheap sleeping bag with both hands to keep some semblance of control. It wasn't just that it had been so long since I'd been with a woman, it was because that she was so instinctively sexy, so beautiful, and everything I ever wanted. Now she was on my living room floor, doing wicked things to my body.

It was almost more than I could take.

She slid further down, then came back up. I shuddered with pleasure as she gently swirled her tongue in circles around me, going further down each time, until she worked her mouth as far down as she could go. She licked the slit dripping with pre-cum, considered the taste, then licked again. "Mmm ... tasty."

She kept her lips soft on the way down and sucked hard as she came back up as if she was milking me for more cum. It was so sexy, such a turn on, that she liked the taste of my cum. I groaned, suddenly on the verge of a humungous climax.

"Do you want me to come inside your mouth or inside your pussy?" I grunted.

"Inside my pussy," she mumbled with her mouth full.

"Then you better fucking stop that, because I can't last much longer," I groaned.

"Okay," she said, but went back down to sucking the hell out of my cock. I closed my eyes and tried to hold off, but fuck me, I was going to explode in her mouth if she carried on one second longer.

"Lara, stop," I growled, grabbing her head.

She released my cock in the most provocative way possible, by running the tip of her tongue all the way upward. Then she sat back and licked her lips. "I didn't know a man's cock could be so delicious," she said cheekily.

I pulled her away from me and set her down beside me. There was a box of condoms somewhere. Were they already expired? Fuck if I knew. It had been a really long time.

"Wait here," I ordered and vaulted upwards. I went to the kitchen, grabbed the box, and as I walked back to the sitting room, pulled one out. As I began to open it, Lara surprised me. "Let me feel what you are doing," she said.

Putting a condom on had never felt so intimate. Her hands were on me as I unrolled it and slipped it on. She helped me pull it down until it was where it belonged, then she excited me by climbing on top. She braced herself with her hands against my shoulders. I pushed up to her, and rubbed my cock against her pussy lips. Instead of pressing down on me, she paused. The first sign of hesitation I had seen from her since she came down to me.

"Lara?"

"I just want you to know that," she whispered, "I've never done this before."

It took a moment for that to sink in. "You've never done what before?" I asked slowly.

"This," she said simply.

I was stunned. What the fuck? She had been so eager and so ... accomplished. I simply took it for granted that she was experienced. The fact that she had never done it with anybody scared the shit out of me. I'd never been the one to make anybody bleed before. Fuck, I'd be fucking a goddamn virgin! But my cock surged even harder, if such a thing were possible at the thought that I would go where no other man had gone.

"Are you sure you want to do this?" I asked her. "Because this is a big thing ... what if you regret this later?"

"I won't," she whispered into my mouth. "I want it to be you."

"It might hurt a little."

"I don't care," she said, and wiggled her hips over me, then slowly began to slide down, taking me one slow inch at a time. I slid my hands over her back, cupped her waist, and slid them down to stroke her hips encouragingly. Curling upwards I gently kissed her neck as she lowered herself onto me. An inch down and she tensed up.

"Oh," she cried.

"It's okay. It'll only hurt for a bit," I encouraged. Her pussy was so hot and tight I had to fight not to cum.

She nodded and pushed another inch down. "Ah," she cried again. Then she took a deep breath and plunged downwards, screaming as she went down my hot girth. She stopped and remained suspended three-quarters of the way down. Sucking in her breath, she put her hands underneath her to feel how much more cock there was too go. To her surprise there was more.

"You don't have to go all the way this time," I soothed.

"Okay," she said. Her voice was hoarse.

"Does it hurt?"

"Yeah. It feels like I've been ripped in half."

"Just move slowly up and down and the pain will go away," I said softly, reaching a hand out to gently stroke her cheek. She was so beautiful. So brave. So perfect. I could hardly believe she was mine.

She began to move slowly and she really was so fucking tight I had to close my eyes and grit my teeth.

"Oh, Kit. It feels good. Really good. I feel so full and so ... stretched," she whispered as she rode me. There was a long sigh from her, but then she slid all the way down, engulfing me completely.

I groaned. My control was already slipping. I could feel the gathering momentum begin, but I wanted to make this good for her. I grabbed her hips and held her still. “Give me a minute,” I hissed through my teeth.

“Is something wrong?” she asked worriedly.

“No. I just need a little break. I’m too close to coming.”

She stayed very still on top of me, and I watched the light dancing on her skin and I thought about what a bastard I was to take her innocence knowing what I knew. It worked. Almost too well. The guilt almost made me go soft.

When I loosened my grip, she began to grind herself on me, moving back and forth. At first her movements were all jerks, stops, and starts, which I was actually grateful for since it made it easier for me to hold my climax, but she quickly got the hang of it, and her rocking became smooth and steady. She leaned forward, and soon she was getting the most out of every stroke. I watched her throw her head back, her mouth open with appreciation. Then she was bouncing on me like someone riding a bull.

“You feel so good,” she panted.

When I couldn’t hold on much longer I reached down between us and touched her clit. She cried out in pleasure, but kept moving while I stroked it in time with her movements. Soon her body began quivering over me as she moved faster and faster. That’s when I joined in, pumping my hips up to meet her while my fingers kept up a steady pace.

“Come for me,” I urged when I felt her pussy squeeze me like a vice.

She suddenly did, with a shout. I grabbed her hips and held her tight against me, letting her little pussy milk me until I sailed right past the point of no return. I came so hard it made me dizzy. The intense pleasure went on and on, longer than it ever had before, and when I opened my eyes Lara collapsed over me, breathing hard, her body still trembling against mine.

"Oh my God," I murmured.

There was that laugh again, bubbling up from deep in her belly. She jerked with laughter as she wrapped her arms around me.

"That was so awesome," she giggled. "How long before we can do it again?"

Twenty-seven

Kit

Pale sun streamed in through the window, waking me up only a few hours after we had finally collapsed with exhaustion. I lay there for a moment, feeling the soreness from muscles that hadn't been used in far too long. Then, almost as if I couldn't quite believe what I would see, I looked over to my right at the most beautiful girl in the world, lying naked in my bed.

The embers in the fireplace weren't quite enough to cut the chill so I had covered her with a heavy quilt. The outline of her strong, lithe body was clear underneath the fabric.

Her bare shoulder peeked out from above the covers, and the sunlight caressed it with a gentle glow. Her hair was mussed, tangled, and falling around her face and shoulders in waves. Her lips were red and swollen with kisses. I remembered again how wonderful she had tasted. Without her glasses to hide her eyes, her eyelashes were incredibly long.

I rolled over as carefully as I could, trying not to disturb her, but I should have known that even as I studied her, she was studying me in her own unique way.

"I've been awake for a while," she whispered, and those plump, red lips curled up into a smile. "I like waking up with you."

"Good," I murmured. "Cause you'll be doing a lot more of it."

"Really?"

"God, yeah."

She giggled and buried her face into the quilt. I slid over and wrapped myself around her. She cuddled into me with an ease that made it feel as though we had done this a million times. My cock started to stir, but I had to tend to the fire first. Naked, I walked to the fireplace and rebuilt it. Then I went back to find her under the quilt.

"Any regrets?" I asked.

She shook her head. "Not a single one. You gave me exactly what I wanted."

"I've never been ... well, you know ... somebody's first."

"Was it what you expected?" she asked shyly.

Huh. What had I expected? I gave it a few moments of thought. "No. It wasn't. I guess I always thought a virgin would be uncertain or wouldn't know what to do, but you ... oh, honey. You're a natural. It's hard to imagine that no other cock has ever entered this sexy mouth. I mean, for a virgin you sure know how to give one hell of a blowjob. What I got last night was porn star quality."

"Elaine," she said, as if that answered everything.

"Elaine?"

"She made me practice on a condom covered banana when we were seventeen."

"I never thought I'd see the day I was jealous of a fucking banana."

She giggled again and buried her head against my neck so I couldn't see her face.

"What? Don't tell me you're embarrassed? After that performance last night. Really?" Women were such funny little creatures. I would never understand them if I lived to a hundred.

"It's one thing to do it and quite another to talk about it," she said primly.

"Hmm ... yes," I teased. "As I recall now, you had no problem doing it. Why you were all over me. Taking advantage of me, really. I mean, even if I had wanted to resist, you were right there on top of me just slamming me into the floor, making sure you got exactly what you wanted. I-"

"Oh, stop being so mean," she laughed.

I laughed along with her. "It's true! I was quite helpless. You were on me like jelly on peanut butter."

Her cheeks became rosy. God, she was so pretty I wanted to lock her up in my house and never let her out.

"Like milk on cereal, your hands and mouth were everywhere," I added, just to see more color flood into her cheeks.

"Stop it," she begged.

I took pity on her. "Oh, babe. You were absolutely amazing last night. Don't you dare be embarrassed about it. I loved it that you were bold and honest and ... so ... lusty."

"You're doing it again," she complained.

I chuckled and caressed her smooth stomach. "All right I'll stop. Are you hungry?"

"I'm starving. Are you?"

"Hell yes," I said, boosting myself up above her. I whipped away the quilt and looked down at my property. Underneath me her legs spread out invitingly. "My, my, look at all this cream. Is it all for me?"

"You're going to eat me again?" she asked shyly.

"Of course. Let me show you just how hungry I am," I growled.

She gave me a dazzling smile and whispered, "Please do."

I reached my hands under her legs and brought them over my shoulders, lifting those bewitching hips right off the bed, and placing my mouth exactly where I wanted it. I blew directly into her little quivering hole, and she squirmed and leaked more thick juice.

"Morning pussy. My favorite," I said, and clamped my mouth over her twitching sex. She grabbed my head and ground my lips into her lovely pussy. I sucked on the engorged clit until it was double the size it was last night. Then, when I had kept her on the edge for so long, she jerked desperately into my mouth.

I bit her clit lightly, and she wrapped her legs around my neck in a vice grip and succumbed to a tremendous screaming climax, gushing sweet fluid into my mouth, over my face, and down my neck.

I grabbed her bottom and kept sucking and licking her pussy, forcing her to cum again. And again. She was begging me to stop as yet another orgasm ripped through her.

By the time I lowered her shaky body down my face and hair were soaked with her juices, and her pussy was swollen and red.

"From now on only I make you cum," I said.

She nodded silently.

"Do you want to sleep for a while"

"I want to drink you the way you drink me," she said breathlessly.

"You want my cum?"

"Yes."

"All right," I said.

Twenty-eight

Lara

It was a long time since Elaine and I practiced on the sheathed banana, but I think I did okay last night, and I was pretty sure I could do it even better today.

Cupping the firm cheeks of his behind, I leaned forward and stretching my lips over his thick hardness, took him into my mouth. Deeper and deeper until he filled my whole mouth and started hitting the back of my throat. I swallowed to keep my gag reflex down, and he groaned with pleasure. There, I just learned something new. The swallowing action was exciting to him.

"Fuck, Lara. Your mouth was made for my cock," he growled.

I tightened my lips around the thick, satin smooth shaft, and he groaned and jerked with pleasure. I could feel his soft curls tickling my face as he started to move his hips as if he was having sex with my mouth. I matched him, by bobbing my head up and down his length faster and faster.

"Lara, wait," he cried, grabbing the sides of my head and firmly holding it still. His thighs and butt were clenched tight.

"What?" I asked around his cock.

"I can't hold on if you go at that speed."

Immediately, I started moving my head up and down his shaft while sucking him harder. I wanted him to lose control. It was an exhilarating sensation to think *I* could drive a man like Kit to such madness.

His cock began to throb and swell, stretching my lips even more. With a primitive roar he suddenly thrust hard into my mouth. I felt hard fast spurts of his warm cum coating my tongue and sliding down my throat. I swallowed every drop of it.

I knew he was watching me and I wanted him to see that I loved his seed. I licked his cock clean, then I gave the tip one last kiss before I sat back down on my calves. He fell backwards and pulled me down with him. I felt the hairs on his chest on my cheeks, and heard the steady thud of his heart.

For a while he was content to simply lie there and hold me. Then I heard the sound of him sheathing himself. Reaching down between us, he grasped my thighs and spread them apart. His hips bucked as the head of his cock pushed at the lips of my sex.

"Fuck you're so wet," he said.

"This time," I whispered. "Don't hold back."

"But that poor pussy must still be tender," he said.

"I like it when you let go completely. Like before. I want you to lose it," I said.

"I'll hurt you. You're so little."

"You won't hurt me. I'm a woman. I'm built to have babies."

"Then I'll take what I need," he growled into my mouth and, rolling me over with his big body, plunged into me. I gasped with the shock of his size.

"Do you want me to slow down?" he asked.

I shook my head. "No, I love being so full of you." I had forgotten how his thickness filled every inch of me. His thrusts were fluid and the pleasure grew in my belly, until it was almost more than I could take.

He started moving faster, pounding deeper with each hard thrust. The harder he slammed into me, the tighter my sex clenched at his shaft. I felt myself start to go over the edge, and my mouth called his name as I climaxed hard and fierce.

"I'm like an animal in heat with you. I want to watch you cum again," he ordered as he rutted with raw need on top of me.

I didn't think I could climax again, but I did. My entire body writhed with ecstasy as a second orgasm rolled over me. After he climaxed we drifted off a bit, halfway between here and dreamland, until he lifted his lips and kissed my chin.

"This feels so damn good. I could stay with my cock parked in your sweet pussy forever."

The grin on my face grew wider. "Free parking. That's considered a good perk for city folk, isn't it?"

"I'd pay everything I own for this parking space."

"You can pay me with food."

"Deal. What do you want? The choice is limited though."

"Can we have pancakes?" I asked with a grin.

"I might have some pancake mix left, but it's almost certainly out of date."

"I'll risk it, if you will."

"You do know that there might only be two flushes left in that toilet until the snow thaws off a bit."

I laughed, but I wouldn't give up on the pancakes.

I wrapped up in his toweling robe and we went into the kitchen and made breakfast together. Well, I made the batter and Kit cooked the pancakes. We brought the food into the living room and ate in front of the fire. He sucked the melted butter and maple syrup off my fingers.

Afterwards, I could barely wait to get dressed and go outside to meet with the wolves again. I hoped Lobo would seek me out once more and show me more affection. I loved the idea that he chose me to be his human!

The air was crisp and frosty, and I stood very still while the wolves milled around Kit. Then, to my delight, a cold nose touched the back of my hand. I caught my breath. Yes, yes, Lobo had come to greet me. He was a big boy. His back came almost to my hips. Very slowly, I reached to the side of him and stroked his pelt. It was thick and dusted with snow.

"Hello, Lobo," I said, crouching down.

Very gently I petted him, and he licked my face. His breath was hot and his tongue rough, and I laughed with the simple joy of having a wild animal lick me. I appreciated that he was feral, but even untamed things have hearts and emotions and know how to love and care. The trust he was showing was sincere. There was no ulterior motive behind it.

Why he picked me, I would never know, perhaps because he accepted me as Kit's mate. I was grateful that he did, and already I loved him. I knew I would treasure him more and more with each passing day.

After a few minutes it seemed he'd had enough of me, and after a final lick, he moved away.

Kit came towards me. "Happy?"

I nodded.

He took my hand and hauled me up so our bodies were touching. "They are your family, aren't they?" I asked.

"Yes."

I understood that simple answer perfectly. There was such a strong bond of uncomplicated love and deep trust that I had never felt the same level while dealing with other humans with their hidden thought processes.

"Is everything covered in snow?" I asked.

"Completely."

"Will you tell me what you see?"

"The whole place is under at least two feet of snow. The wolves are playing on the freshly fallen snow, and leaving their funny little trails. Oh, and there's an eagle in the sky now."

"An eagle," I cried eagerly.

"Yeah, I think he has a nest in a tree very near here, because he seems to hang around a lot.

Sometimes he perches right up at the top of the tallest pine on your left. He is so big and solid he looks like his weight could bend the branches over, but in fact, he sits so lightly up there he doesn't even shake the snow off. He always looks as if he's poised to dive down on the next big air current.

"Sometimes he will spread his wings very slowly. If you were a fool you'd think he was lazy, but if you had a spoonful of wits about you, you'd know, he's a cunning old buzzard, and you'd be right too. I've seen him bend his wings all the way back, then before I could blink he'd plunged towards the ground, so damn fast it was like someone shot him out of that tree.

"There was a sudden panic and chaos on the ground, then I was watching the strength in his back as he swooped away with some small creature so terrified and shocked it was frozen."

"What's he doing now?"

"He's sitting perfectly still and looking right back at us."

The rest of the day was a dream. We went back inside and made love by the fire. Then I waited inside while Kit shoveled snow and freed the pickup.

That evening I cooked rabbit stew. It was great food for a cold night. We just talked for hours. Kit wanted to know everything about me. I learned that there are some parts of Kit that made him clam up. Then the atmosphere would change, become tense and sometimes even sad.

I told myself I would heal him. One day I would heal him.

Twenty-nine

Lara

https://www.youtube.com/watch?v=zoENAD7OCiI

"Where were you yesterday and this morning?" Elaine demanded fiercely. "I called, and called, but there was no reply."

I grinned. "At Kit's."

"What do you mean at Kit's?"

"We did it, Elaine," I whispered.

"What?" she yelled.

"Shhh …" crusty old Mister Sullivan scolded, flapping his loose lips together.

"Oh! Shhh yourself," Elaine exclaimed rudely, before turning to me and whispering urgently, "You didn't?"

"I sure did," I confirmed firmly.

"No," she gasped in her most scandalized voice.

I nodded.

"You can't have. I don't believe it."

I nodded more vigorously. "It's just like you said, Elaine. Out of this world. I thought I was falling into a void. It was just so amazing."

Elaine leaned forward. "Oh! My! God! You're serious, aren't you? You got your V card punched!"

I grinned happily. “I think I’m in love.”

“Stop being so sappy. You are not in love. It’s just sex. You’ll get over it.”

“It’s not just the sex. I just feel something here.” I touched the area over my heart.

“Like how you felt about Sawyer?” she asked sarcastically.

I frowned and shook my head. “No, not like that. That was just a childish crush. I was a girl then. What I feel for Kit is totally different.”

“Really? What do you feel?” Her voice bristled with naked curiosity.

“When he touches me, it feels as if I’ll go up in flames.”

Elaine laughed. “That’s called lust, honey.”

“Shhh ...” Mister Sullivan hissed again.

“Oh, for crying out loud. Have you not gone home yet?” she asked, completely irritated.

“I’m trying to read the paper here,” he grumbled.

“Well, switch off your hearing aids and get on with it then,” she snapped.

“It’s not lust,” I insisted. “I feel ... connected to him. As if I belong to him and he to me. It’s like I’ve been looking for him all my life.”

Elaine stiffened suddenly.

“What?” I asked.

“You’ll never believe who just walked in here.”

“Who?” I whispered, my own back tensed and straight.

She didn’t need to speak. I knew exactly who was behind me. Citrus and rosemary cologne filled my nostrils. I turned around. “Hello, Sawyer.”

“Hello, Lara. Elaine.”

“Hey, Sawyer. How are things going?” Elaine asked in her fake saccharine voice.

“Great, thanks.”

“How’s Kayleigh?”

“Yeah, she’s fine.” His voice was tight and strained. Oh, mistake, mistake. Elaine could scent a good gossip from miles away.

“The wedding is soon, isn’t it?” Elaine asked, switching to her you-can-tell-me-anything-cause-I’m-your-good-friend voice.

“July.” His voice was as clipped as his answer.

“I bet Kayleigh must be right busy with all the preparations,” she said so innocently, you’d swear butter wouldn’t melt in her mouth.

“She is.”

“Where is she now, anyway?”

“New York.”

“Kleinfeld?” she guessed, her voice riding a few octaves higher.

“Yes.”

“Oh my, how exciting! Has she already picked out her dress?”

“Err ... no ... I mean. I’m not sure if she’s decided yet.” He cleared his throat. “Can I have a word, Lara?”

I smiled even though I was furious with him. How dare he approach me here in the library? He knew this place was crawling with gossipers so I’d be forced to talk to him, or risk being labeled as the Scarlet woman trying to break up the most anticipated wedding of the century.

"Of course. Did you want help with the wedding?" I asked politely.

"Outside, please."

I frowned. He wasn't even attempting to pretend. "Right. If you lead the way." I turned to face Elaine and said loudly enough for Mister Sullivan to hear. I notice that he had stopped asking us to Shhh. "This shouldn't take long, Elaine. I'm just helping Sawyer with the present for the bride."

We went outside with me walking, stiff as a board, behind him. I heard the door close. A gust of cold wind blew into my face. "What do you want?" I demanded frostily.

"I know you stayed at his house during the blizzard," he accused as if he had the right.

"Sawyer," I gritted, barely holding on to my temper, "I don't have to account my movements to you."

"Just tell me he didn't take advantage of you."

The vortex of fury in my chest grew. "I'm not telling you anything. It's none of your business."

He made an anguished sound. "Oh my God! He did, didn't he? I'll kill him."

"How dare you?" I began, my hands were trembling with frustration, but he was in full flow.

"You gave what was mine to him," he seethed. "How could you? You know I love you. I'll see him in a cold meat wagon before I let him have you. You're mine, Lara. I'll show him. I'll show that ugly bastard." He turned and walked away from me.

For a second I stood at the top of the steps, not moving, my mouth open, astonished by the fierce malice and rage in his voice. I never realized such strong emotion existed within him. As a matter of fact, I didn't think anyone suspected him capable of such feelings. He was so soft and gentle Elaine once called him the 'nutless wonder'. Surely he couldn't be the sweet man who let me feel his handsome face with my fingers. I still had the bust I made of him hidden away in my cupboard. I would have to take it out and destroy it; I no longer wanted it. A shiver went over me.

While I was standing there, frozen with shock, I heard footsteps coming up the pavement. They stopped at the bottom of the stairs, and then came up the steps. Vanilla mixed with rose scented face powder. My heart sank. Of all the people I would have to meet just at that crazy surreal moment it had to be dyed-in-the-wool doomsayer, Marybeth Luther.

I schooled my features, and prayed she had not heard Sawyer's parting threat. Taking a deep breath, I turned towards her with a friendly smile. "Hello, Mrs. Luther." To my horror my voice was shaking.

"Don't you Hello me, Missie. Your disgraceful goings on have reached my ears." She harrumphed.

"What disgraceful goings on?" I asked.

She snorted. “Play the innocent with someone else. I know what’s going on. You’ve taken up with that heathen beast in the forest.”

“He’s not a heathen beast. He’s a good man,” I defended automatically.

“A good man? He’s never set foot in our church. There’s a place in hell for men like him,” she huffed.

Another time I wouldn’t have reacted to her sanctimonious preaching and scolding, but after what Sawyer just put me through, I couldn’t take it lying down. “Well, then I’m going to the same place because I got naked with him,” I confessed hotly.

Her gasp of shock at my confession exhilarated me.

“Lara Jane Young,” she breathed, her hand hitting her heart with a soft thud. “What on earth has gotten into you? That’s a shameful, disgraceful thing to say.”

“Why?”

“Well, it’s just not Christian,” she blustered.

That made me even more angry. Who was she to tell me how Christian I was? “Is that what the phrase, ‘Yes, they’ll know we are Christians by our love,’ means when you sing it at the top of your voice from the front row of church every Sunday?”

“I promised your poor mother, God bless her soul, before she went to meet our Heavenly Father that I’d keep an eye on you. She’ll be turning in her grave to know what you’re up to, young lady.”

“My mother would have been pleased to make the acquaintance of such a gentleman as Kit

Carson. Now, if you'll excuse me I'm late," I said as regally as I could, and began to walk down the steps. There was fresh snow on top of the ice so I took my steps carefully. Falling flat on my face was not the dramatic exit I wanted to make.

"Mark my words, child. Stop this madness now, or you'll be sorry."

I turned around slowly. The snow under my foot crunching. I was determined not to let anyone bully me. I knew what I wanted and I refused to cower to anyone in this matter. "No, I won't," I said clearly. "And I'm not a child. He's a beautiful man. You just can't see it because you're only looking with your eyes."

That shut her up.

I walked over to the grocery store to buy apples, ranch dressing, pop rocks, and canned pumpkin. I was planning to make a pie to take with me to Kit's.

Daisy, the bubblegum chewing cashier was a bit funny with me as she rang me up. I guess the whole town had heard. I spent the night in the forest with the heathen beast.

Thirty

Kit

https://www.youtube.com/watch?v=oKnMK-eqKfM

Until you've walked in someone else's shoes ...

It may be a cliché, but it sure as hell was true. I wanted to walk in Lara's shoes. To know and experience the darkness intimately, the way she did. I wrapped an arm under her and the other across the back of her thighs and swooped her into my arms.

"What are you doing Kit?"

"You'll see." I said as I hurried her upstairs. My cock was already barely able to restrain itself inside my pants. I went straight to the bedroom and put her down.

"Tell me," she begged.

"I want us to fuck in complete darkness."

"Well that's easy. Lara chuckled. "I always do it in the dark."

"Exactly, and I want to experience how that feels."

"Why?"

"Because I want to know what you feel," I said.

A cheeky grin lit up her face. "Well what are you waiting for then?"

“Wait,” I said, and opening a drawer found an old scarf. I folded it into a thick band and walked back to her. “Tie this around my eyes.

She placed it over my eyes and tightened the knot behind my head. “How's that?”

“I can't see a thing.”

“Great, since that was kinda the point.”

“Come here,” I called, and heard her walking around me. When she stood in front of me, I pulled her tightly against my body. My dick throbbed as my mouth eagerly searched her out. The kiss deepened, in the darkness our mouths hungrily devouring each other. We were like wild animals.

Our mouths fused. Lost in the smell and feel of her, I walked her backwards in the direction of the bed. The backs of her legs met the bed and I sat her down on it.

Grasping the bottom of her dress, I pulled it upwards until it cleared her head. I flung it to one side. I brushed strands of hair out of her face, marveling at its soft silky texture. I reached behind her, unbuckled her bra and let it slip down her body. I let my rough palms graze the tips of her breasts. They were like hard pebbles. Her skin was softer than I remembered.

She arched her body to meet mine.

My cock was aching, but I wasn't ready to take her yet. I quickly dragged off my shirt. I found myself enjoying the ragged sound of our breathing. Her hands came up to feel my chest, but I pushed her back on the soft covers.

She sighed.

"Shhh, baby. I've got you so go ahead and be as shameless as you want. Lie back and spread your legs as wide as you can for me. I heard the sheets rustle as she obeyed my instruction. I crouched between her legs. I couldn't see her pretty little pussy, but I could smell it. And it was even sweeter. She still had her thong on, and I grazed my fingertip on the crotch. It was deliciously wet. Gently I dropped my lips onto the thinly covered folds, blowing my hot breath on the sweet pea underneath.

She writhed with pleasure.

"Push your pussy into my mouth. Show me how horny you are," I instructed.

"Okay," she whispered.

I heard her hips rise off the bed, searching for my mouth. When it connected, she gasped.

"Show me how much you want it."

The silky material rustled as she pushed it to one side with her fingers. With a soft moan, she pushed her naked pussy on my mouth and moved her hips up and down, so that my tongue was dragged back and forth over her puffy folds. Back and forth. Back and forth. Her breaths were like an orchestra in my ears, highs and lows.

She was such a tease she would have carried on longer, but there was only so much I could take. I was only a man. I grabbed her hips and drew the whole thing in my mouth and sucked it hungrily. She screamed. Her cream ran down my throat. The more she creamed, the more I feasted on all that tasty goodness, until she was as mad for me to take her as I was.

“Please, please,” she begged, digging her fingers into my hair. “I can’t take much more.”

Her soaked thong rubbed against my cheek. My teeth tore the damn thing right off her body in one swipe and tossed it aside. My greedy girl’s hips were rising off the bed to encourage me to slide my fingers into her.

I didn’t.

I rose up and joined her on the bed. Crawling alongside her, I kissed her soft skin as I made my way up her body. Her thighs, the swell of her stomach, the roundness of her breasts, her exposed throat. It was a treasure trove of delight, and it was all mine.

She made little kitten sounds of pure pleasure. Then, when she least expected it, I latched onto her clit, and sucked hard. I didn’t let go until I felt her lower body clench as a massive climax roared through her.

I'd never imagined just how sensuous and sexy it was to control a woman's body that you couldn’t see; only smell, feel and hear, as she began the journey to a climax that ended with her screaming. Without my sight her shout seemed louder, the pitch higher. My cock was weeping in my pants.

“Your turn now,” she whispered.

“That’s right baby girl, it’s *my* turn now, and I’ve got a cock full of cum for little pussy."

She giggled. “Is that so?” she asked playfully.

She wasn’t going to be playful for long. I was planning on hearing her scream the house down. I yanked off my jeans and set my cock free. I straddled Lara's slim body and slid my fingers down it so they would act as my eyes.

My cock grazed her stomach. Her instinctive reaction was to reach down, grasp my hardness between both hands, and stroke it. Her hands were warm and soft and I thought I'd come right there in her grip. I leaned forward and with surprising accuracy, caught her bottom lip between my teeth. I swallowed her gasp of surprise. I was getting good at knowing my lover.

Using my hands, I stretched her legs apart as far as possible and fed my cock into her open pussy. I felt like a beast claiming its mate.

"Jesus Lara, you're so fucking tight," I whispered into her mouth.

"I can feel your cock throbbing and pulsating inside me," she said in wonder. You know what. I could feel her pussy walls grabbing me like a vice. It was fucking beautiful. She was mine. All mine. I didn't need to see to know that. Her body told me all I needed to know with every tremor, every sigh, every beat.

Surrounded by the sound of our bodies slapping against each other and our heartbeats in my head I, pumped into her. The smell of sex filled my nostrils as I rammed my bone as far into her as possible. My Lara found space for every inch. I rocked, twisted and plunged into her as she shouted. "I'm coming, Kit." we both held on tight as she milked me of every last drop of seed I could muster. Her hot juices drenched my thighs.

I stayed inside her, enjoying the sensation of our mating, until the sweat had dried on my body and our breathing returned to normal. I didn't take the blindfold off even after I pulled out of her body. We lay with my big leg across her stomach, and my arms around her. Lara turned to me.

"Whoa Kit, that was magical. I think I'll keep you blindfolded a lot more often."

"I think I'd like that."

We laughed into the quiet night.

Thirty-one

Lara

"Elaine, I'm going on a date."

"Amputate your timber!" she squealed gleefully.

I laughed.

"Where to?" she asked eagerly.

"I don't know yet, but somewhere out of town."

"What're you fixin' to wear?"

"I don't know. Mom always said the dress with the square neckline suited me best."

"The green one with the A line skirt? Yeah, I like that on you, but I think we probably need something a bit more special than that. My sister has got something really nice. I'll ask her if you can wear it. I'm sure she'll say yes."

"What is it?"

"It's a knee-length, long sleeved, red dress, but it's form fitting and very glamorous. You'll look great in it. What about shoes? You're not going to wear your usual clodhoppers, are you?"

"I've ballet flats."

"Nah, they won't look good with the red dress. Haven't you got those delicate kitten heels that we bought together at Wapleys?"

"I do, but I could also fall and break my neck if I wear them in this weather."

“Okay, scrap that idea. How about the boots that you wore for Bobby Dearfield’s funeral?”

“They kinda pinch my toes.”

“So what? It’s not like you’ll be walking to the restaurant. You’ve never suffered for beauty. It’s time you did,” she said callously.

“I guess I could wear that if you think it will look best.”

“I do. Are you putting your hair up?”

“Should I?” I asked uncertainly.

“Hmm ... down. It’s sexier.”

I giggled. “I’m actually getting a bit nervous about it all. I’ve never been out on a date before.”

“Aren’t you forgetting Peter Wheeler?”

“Peter? Have you forgotten? His mother forced him to take me to the dance because she thought it was the Christian thing to do. I don’t think he even wanted to be seen with me. It was so awkward. Poor guy couldn’t wait to drop me off.”

“The nerve of some people. It’s not like he’s the catch of the century. There was a reason why everybody called him Picket Fence Peter in school.”

I missed out on so much by being homeschooled. “Picket Fence Peter?”

“With buck teeth like his he could have eaten apples through a picket fence.”

I smiled. “Really. I didn’t even know he had buck teeth.”

“Worse than Bugs Bunny. Anyway, there’s nothing to be nervous about. It’s not an exam. Besides you’ve already done the deed. Just relax, eat some chow, down a couple of glasses of wine, and have fun."

"Elaine?"

"Yeah."

"Will you come over and slap some make-up on me?"

"Oh, honey. Of course I will," Elaine said, an odd catch in her voice.

"The thing is I don't have any," I confessed.

"I know that, ducky. Don't you worry none. I'll bring my whole collection of Maybe it's Maybelline for you," she assured immediately.

"Thank you, Elaine."

"Remember all those times I made you jump puddles that weren't there?"

"Yeah."

"Tonight I'll make you look so beautiful, it'll make up for all that jumping for no reason."

Elaine came more than an hour before my date. She let herself in with her key and came upstairs to sit at the edge of my bath.

"What's that smell?" I asked.

"Shine," she replied with a laugh.

"Where on earth did you get that from?"

"Got it for a steal from Catfish Colter."

"Is it any good?" I asked holding my hand out.

She fitted a glass into my outstretched hand and I curled my fingers around it. "It'll burn your insides and probably damage your liver for good, but it's darn good stuff."

She was right about burning my insides, hopefully not about the second part. Still, we had a giggly glass together while she painted my face. I was not used to drinking and I was quite tipsy by the time she stood back from me and said, "Poor Sawyer. He sure got the wrong pig by the tail by picking Kayleigh over you."

"Sawyer was never sweet on me," I denied immediately. Even though I was angry with Sawyer I didn't want the whole town gossiping about him and me.

"Never sweet on you? Don't piss on my leg and tell me it's raining," she scoffed.

"Anyway," I said firmly. "He loves Kayleigh now and all is well that ends well." I was never revealing to Elaine how savagely he had threatened "to show" Kit. Even I found it hard to believe that I hadn't just dreamed it all up.

"Well, good luck to him is what I say," she muttered darkly. "He's climbing a barbed wire fence naked."

"Why do you say that?" I asked, very curious as to why she would say something so ominous.

"Last I heard Kayleigh has her Daddy all twisted up around her little finger, and Rhett Haverbrooke is one tall barbed wire fence. If Sawyer's got any plans of not being the dream husband Kayleigh wants, he'll be in shreds by the time he gets over on the other side."

"What makes you think Sawyer wants to get to the other side?"

"His edgy smile," she said confidently. That was the thing about Elaine. Not much escaped her sharp eyes.

"You think he's marrying her for her money, don't you?" I asked slowly.

"Sawyer Buchanan wants Kayleigh Haverbrooke as much as you'll be wanting your nightshirt tonight."

In spite of a nagging worry about Sawyer and his furious hiss, I had to laugh at her extremely accurate comment.

Thirty-two

Lara

Elaine left about ten minutes before Kit was due to arrive.

I practiced walking about in my black boots, and it wasn't so bad. Elaine had persuaded me to wear stockings so it didn't chaff too bad. When the doorbell rang I could hear my heart pounding in my ears as I walked to it.

I opened it to Kit's sharply indrawn breath, and the smell of clean soap and mothballs. He must have dug out some long unused clothes from his cupboard.

"Wow," he exclaimed.

"Elaine, you know, my best friend, I told you about her, made me up," I babbled with a big grin.

"You look amazing."

I wrinkled my nose. "You smell of mothballs."

"Sorry."

"I don't know. I've always been a bit of sucker for the smell of mothballs. Mmmm."

He reached forward, and cupping my buttocks with his large, calloused hands, pulled me close to his body. His body was warm, and the buttons on his shirt pressed into me. "Did somebody say something about sucking?" he asked.

"I might have mentioned it," I whispered. This close I could smell his skin. My stomach tightened.

He kissed me long and lingeringly, and I felt my blood pulsing in my veins, and my stomach clench tightly. In his arms my body began to shiver with desire. Just when I thought my whole soul would be laid bare to him, he raised his head and whispered, "Do you know I'm batshit crazy about your scent? It's fucking driving me insane. Aren't you wearing pants, or something?"

I giggled. "You don't think I would be that naughty, do you?"

He rubbed his hands sensuously around my butt cheeks, then stopped and said, incredulously, "You little tease. You're not wearing any, are you?"

"Nope."

He groaned. "Fuck, how am I supposed to eat knowing you've gone commando? Did I just feel the garters of your stocking against my leg?"

"Obviously, since I'm planning on seducing you tonight."

"The only one seducing anyone tonight, will be me. Guess what I'm going to do to you this fine night?"

My cheeks burned. "I don't know. What?"

"I'm gonna open your legs and make full use of my free parking permit for hours and hours."

"You are a wild and wicked man, Kit Carson," I mock-scolded while grinning stupidly up at him. Nobody had ever wanted me like this. Despite the fact that Sawyer seemed to have developed some kind of creepy possessiveness all of a sudden, until now, nobody wanted the blind girl. I was more like the town mascot. A way for them to feel good about themselves. No matter how bad things got at least, thank God, they still had their sight. Not like poor Lara, living all alone in darkness.

“Do you want to come in?” I asked.

“Do I ever?” he said. Without letting go of my body, he walked me backwards and shut the door with his foot.

“Want a drink? Elaine brought a bottle of shine, and there’s still some left.”

“Nope. I want to see your studio.”

I was suddenly shy. “Oh! Uh ... it might not be your thing.”

“I don’t have much time for art, but I do want to see what *you*’ve created. It’ll be like peeking into your head.”

I bit my bottom lip. “Okay, but you don’t have to pretend you like it or anything like that if you don’t. I’m all right with the fact that it might not be to your taste.”

“You’ll never catch me pretending anything,” he said softly, almost absently, while his finger lightly stroked my cheek.

I took a step back from him, and squaring my shoulders led the way.

“Jesus, that’s some dress you have on. Even the back view is giving me a hard on,” he growled behind me.

I laughed and kept walking as if I was sophisticated and had men say such risqué things to me all the time, but there was more sway to my hips than there was before. It was quite amazing how quickly I had become such a sexual creature after a lifetime of being completely sexless.

At the door to my studio, I hesitated.

"I'm gonna have to see some day," he whispered close to my ear.

I turned the knob and entered, knowing the first thing he would see would be Ella, my mermaid. No one, not even Elaine, had laid an eye on her yet. She was the biggest project I'd ever attempted. I knew in my heart that she was the best thing I had ever done, but that made me nervous as hell that she might not be as good as I thought she was. "This is Ella. She's not completely finished yet. The rock she is sitting on still needs to be polished and painted," I said nervously.

"Where's the light switch?" he asked.

"Oh, of course." I whirled around, fumbled at the wall and switched the light on. I hadn't used it in years, and hoped it still worked.

He gasped behind me. I stood very still, and listened to him walk towards my mermaid.

"My God, Lara, this is ... it's ... just ... superb. Wow, I never imagined something so magical ... and the colors, how? Wow."

I heard him walk around the sculpture, then stop, and turn towards me. "You saw this in your head?"

I shrugged. "Yeah."

"But the colors? They match and blend. How did you?" He seemed amazed.

I shrugged. "That's the way my mind thinks a mermaid should look."

“It’s incredible, Lara,” he said sincerely. “I don’t know what I expected, but not this. I wouldn’t even have expected something so accomplished from someone with sight, but someone who lived in darkness. It’s pure genius.”

He walked up to me. His wonderful scent filled my nostrils as I buried my face in his neck. “Thank you,” I whispered.

“No, thank you.”

“For what?”

“For being so beautiful.”

“I’m not beautiful,” I said automatically.

“Shall I let you see what I am looking at?”

“Okay.”

“Elaine has painted your eyes so they look really big. Your cheeks are pink, and your mouth is the same color as the ripest, most delicious strawberry. It is slightly open as if it is begging for a kiss ... or my cock.”

“Or food,” I said cheekily.

He laughed, a rich, deep sound. “Come on, little minx,” he said, putting his arm under my hand.

He helped me into my coat and buttoned me in. It was lovely to feel so protected and safe. I locked my door and we walked down the path together. It was cold and I was careful in my black boots. He put me in the truck, closed the door, and went around to the driver’s side.

Thirty-three

Lara

"Where are you taking me?" I asked.

"It's in Charlottesville and it's called Camel Hump Grille, but don't let the name put you off."

I laughed. "I've been to Charlottesville with Elaine, but I've never heard of a restaurant called Camel Hump Grille."

"It's small and it's almost just a roadside shack, but they do one heck of a steak. Their dry aged cuts are almost a legend."

Camel Hump Grille was more than an hour away. He parked and came around to let me out. As I turned to get down, Kit curled his hands around my waist and lifted me down to the blacktop. I took a deep breath. My stomach was full of fluttering butterflies. I put my palm against it.

He had gone very still. "What are you doing?" I asked.

"Just gawking at you."

"I'm actually a bit nervous, Kit."

"Don't be. You look absolutely beautiful. If I can walk into that place with my charred face you can definitely go in looking like a million dollars."

I smiled up at him. "Ma used to say I was pretty, but nobody's called me beautiful before."

“Then they’re all blind as bats,” he said firmly.

I laughed and hooked my hand through his. Kit made me happy. When I was with him I forgot I was considered disabled by the world around me. We walked into the restaurant together; his body warm against mine.

The restaurant was full of noise, people talking, laughing, cutlery, footsteps, children’s voices, music, and more. The smell of food mingled with that of perfume, deodorants and aftershaves. A woman greeted us cheerfully, took our coats, and showed us to our table.

It took a moment to realize the seating was banquette style. As I slid along the curving leather seat, I felt Kit’s muscular thigh slide flush against mine from the opposite side.

He ran his hand up the inside of my leg making my skin tingle. A waitress brought menus, but Kit said we had no need for them. We were there for Boone’s big ole steaks. He told the waitress he wanted his so rare he might as well go up to a cow and bite its butt. I heard the waitress’s pen scratching as she wrote down bloody and medium on her notepad. I ordered a glass of wine, and Kit got himself a cold beer. Then we talked. Unimportant things. He told me he was allergic to the smell of soy sauce and I told him I couldn’t eat spaghetti.

“Why?” he asked.

“Because it feels shockingly similar to slimy worms, and I can’t imagine that it could possibly taste good.”

He chuckled. "You don't know what you're missing."

"Thanks, but I'll pass," I said.

Then he told me about the time he was so drunk he almost had sex in a public toilet with a man dressed as a woman. The way he described his reaction when he reached between 'her' legs and found things he did not think was funny, had me laughing uproariously.

Then I told him about the time a bird pooped on my head and I couldn't figure what it was that fell on me. I thought he would laugh, but he leaned in and sighed almost wishfully, "Oh, Lara. How different the world is for you."

"What are you afraid of?" I asked him.

"I'm afraid of ... I'm afraid only of losing you," he said softly.

"Why would you lose me? You can see," I quipped.

He didn't laugh. "No matter what happens, just know that you are the most important thing that ever happened to me," he said.

I wanted to tell him then that I loved him, but the food arrived. In the flurry about forks and knives and instructions about where everything was, the moment was lost.

The steak was juicy and delicious, but it was so massive I couldn't finish it. We had apple pie for dessert. It was okay, but Elaine's grandma's pie would have knocked spots off theirs. Neither of us wanted coffee so Kit paid the bill and we left.

It was snowing again. The flakes were coming down fast. They fell softly on my face.

“Shit,” Kit cursed. “You’ll be able to drive as well as me in this weather.”

I was still laughing when he bundled me into the truck. I rubbed my hands together to warm them. Kit had brought blankets and he wrapped my legs in them.

“Thank you,” I whispered.

“I guessed you’d be wearing a skirt,” he said gruffly, and I marveled at how thoughtful he was.

After a while the heating from the heater kicked in. I felt warm, cozy and deliciously drowsy after all the wine and food, and I fell asleep on his shoulder.

I woke up to a soft kiss on my lips. Then another. And another. The last one was deeper, lasted longer. I moaned with pleasure.

“This is the way everyone should be woken up,” I sighed.

He chuckled. “We’re home, baby.”

That made me smile. He was calling his home mine as well. “I’m home when I’m in your arms,” I whispered.

“Want me to carry you in?”

“And have you fall and drop me in the snow? No thanks,” I said with a giggle.

“Very funny,” he said, and hopped out of the truck. Before I knew it, strong arms were hooking themselves under my knees and neck and I was being hoisted out and held close to a warm, hard body.

"You're going to chuck me in the snow, aren't you?"

"Nah, I have a better plan," he said, walking up the driveway.

He never locked his door so he just kicked it open, and kicked it shut again. He swept me through the hallway and up the stairs as if I was some heroine in a romantic movie. I never realized that there was something so primitive and wonderful about a large and powerful man who picks you up and carries you to his bed. He threw me on the bed.

"Hey," I protested, but he already had grabbed my ankles and opened my legs. For a while he seemed to do nothing. "What are you doing?" I asked.

"Just looking at my sweet pussy. I missed her all day."

Then I heard him take off his clothes and the rustle of a condom wrapper. The mattress gave way as he lay down on the bed. He curled his large hands around my waist and picked me up, depositing me on his lap, facing him, my legs spread apart.

"Show me your pussy."

I reached for the hem of my dress to pull it over my head, but he stopped me.

"No, not all the way. I've been dying to fuck you in that dress." He scrunched it up until it was between my waist and my hips.

"Spread your thighs wider," he instructed.

I leaned back on his raised thighs and opened my legs as wide as I could.

His hand reached out and touched my sex. "Fuck, you're so wet. You have no idea how pink and delicious you look, do you?"

I shook my head.

Gently he rubbed my sex in slow circles; I moaned and rocked my hips. He inserted a long finger deep into me and my head dropped back with pleasure.

"Do you know what I'm doing?"

I shook my head.

"I'm finger fucking you."

"That sounds really dirty," I gasped.

"That's because it is really dirty. My finger is going in and out of your tight, wet pussy. Every time I go in, your pussy sucks me in eagerly, and every time I come out, she makes a popping sound, and begs me for more. What do you think she's really begging for, Lara?" As he asked he slipped two fingers into me

"Your cock?" I groaned.

"Why my cock?"

"Because it feels good when you fill me up."

He lifted my body with his hands as if I weighed no more than a feather. "You are so little, Lara," he crooned as he positioned me over his cock. "I'm sometimes afraid of hurting you."

"I told you before. I don't want you to be careful. I want you to go crazy."

I felt the head of his shaft push past my soaked folds and penetrate me, stretching me. My muscles immediately started to squeeze at the invading body.

"See how she is trying to suck my cock in," he marveled.

More of his meat entered me as he pushed me further down his shaft. As my muscles stretched and adjusted to his size, I began to wriggle so that more and more of him slipped deeper into me. My open pussy was almost sitting on his crotch. It felt as if I was as stuffed as one of Elaine's grandmother's Thanksgiving turkeys.

"I still don't fit yet, do I?" I whispered.

"You will. You're small and tight, but you'll get used to my size. You'll take everything I've got. Soon."

He was willing to wait, but I wasn't. I wanted all of him. *Now*. I started moving on him. First short strokes then longer and longer ones. I was determined to take all of him that night, for us to fit perfectly. I began to slide down faster and faster. It hurt a bit, but there was more pleasure in knowing that soon he would fit perfectly inside me.

He started to match my thrusts with his own. Our mating became more frenzied, more uncontrollable. Strange sounds of pleasure were ripped from me. When a two-pronged slam brought me all the way down to his pubic bone, I screamed with pleasure. We were an exact fit. Like two pieces of a puzzle we fit exactly with not a millimeter to spare.

With a shudder I went over the edge.

When Kit climaxed he roared my name and I moaned for the fact that his seed did not spill into my body. I decided then he would never again wear a sheath with me. I wanted his seed. I wanted him to be mine for keeps. Forever. I wanted to bear his children.

With a sigh of contentment, I arched my head back as his tongue trailed fire down my throat, and prepared myself to feel the climax rise from deep inside me.

Thirty-four

Kit

https://www.youtube.com/watch?v=orkEnnQN5wM

I heard the sound while I was still asleep. Somebody who didn't know better would have called it a thump, but I knew better. It was a noise that you never forgot once you heard it. Even in my dream I became uneasy. My gut was roiling, like the boiling contents of a cauldron.

That sound didn't belong in my dream. I was in a garden. My wolves were there. So was Lara. We were eating. Chepi was lying in my lap and I was stroking Lara's hair.

The next sound made the hair at the back of my neck stand. I recognized that sound too. In my dream I turned to Lara and she was fading, her face was melting. I fought my way out of my dream, and my eyes snapped open.

Every survival instinct I had was on high alert. I jackknifed upwards, alarm bells going off in my brain, adrenaline rushing through my veins. Something was wrong. I glanced down. Lara was still asleep. I pushed the blankets back.

"What's wrong?" Lara's sleepy voice mumbled as her hand stretched out to feel for me.

"Nothing," I lied. "Go back to sleep." I jumped out of bed and landed on the floor like a cat, ready for trouble.

"Where're you going?" she asked.

"Don't leave this room until I come back," I ordered, and moved to pick up my trousers.

Then I heard another sound, and my body went crazy. That was no fucking dream. I stopped thinking. I became an animal. Stark naked, I grabbed my pistol from the top of the dresser, and I ran as fast as my feet could carry me. I rushed down the stairs, and flinging open the front door, I burst out into the porch. Frigid air filled my lungs and gripped my body in an icy clench, but I was so hyped up I didn't even feel it.

There was half a moon in the sky, and it lit up the white ground like a lantern. Everything was eerily still as I'd stood there surveying the open ground. Not a soul anywhere, but there were trails on the snow. My animals. They had scattered in all directions. I went down the steps on my bare feet, my eyes moving, searching. Then I saw the dark shape in the snow, moving towards me.

I raced towards it.

The whole time my mind was screaming no, no, no. I stopped a few feet from the dark shadow and looked at it in disbelief.

"No." The sound was wrenched from deep inside me. "Oh my God, no."

The pistol fell from my nerveless hands. I dropped to my knees. "No, no, no, please, please. No."

My beautiful, beautiful girl. Oh, Chepi, no. Why? Why? Why? Tears filled my eyes and ran down my face. I crawled to her body, sobbing like a child. An arrow protruded from the area near her heart. It was embedded a good five inches inside her. Her coat was soaked in dark blood and more was pouring out of her, but I didn't see what you or anybody else would have seen. I saw an archer saying, "Hey, Wolf. Taste the rainbow. Not quite a dead center, heart shot, couple of inches out, but still a good kill shot, dude."

I had reached her in time to watch the fierce green fire die in her eyes. She was mortally wounded, but there was no revenge, hatred, or malice in her eyes. She could not focus properly on me. Her poor body had gone into convulsions. Her mouth was open, but no sound was coming from it.

I realized there was nothing I could do for her, but offer her an escape from her terrible pain.

I reached down and kissed her cheek, I swear her eyes swiveled and looked at me. In that moment we learned more about each other than ever before. I couldn't remember the last time I'd shed a tear, but I couldn't stop them pouring down my eyes. We both knew in that moment what needed to be done.

She was ready to go.

She had crawled as far as her wounded body would allow her to, to get back to me. Now it was my turn.

"My brave Cepti. Don't you worry none. I'll take care of everything. No more suffering for my beautiful girl."

I swallowed my pain, lifted her head, and snapped her neck quickly like it was a twig.

Her lifeless body lay in my hands. It had been years since I'd lost anyone of value in my life, and I'd almost forgotten how that felt. Now I'd lost one of my family. The pain was indescribable. Chepi was young and so full of vigor I had even imagined she'd outlive me, and worried what would happen to her when I was gone, but she'd been cruelly robbed of her best years.

Suddenly, the pain was too much and I roared an almighty scream of anguish. I'd dabbed the tears away and with my almost frozen crimson hand, I yanked the arrow in one clean thrust out of her chest. Her blood was already becoming solid in the freezing temperatures.

For a second I stared at the arrow. A Tac arrow!

I knew then this was no accidental killing. Whoever shot Chepi was a professional hunter with one of the most expensive and accurate crossbows available. Its bolt speed is so incredible that no animal in the world would have time to react before it hit. Its power was such that it would penetrate any fatty tissue and shatter any bones in its way at eighty plus yards.

Considering it had felled a wolf, it was probably a PSE Tac Elite. My grief quickly turned to the kind of black rage that completely engulfed my senses. An owl hooted back in the spruce, a tree cracked sharply with the frost as the rest of my family members started appearing all around me. Andak, Adam, Rolak, Koa, Lobo ...

One by one they had come to pay their last respects. I heard a sound and whirled around, more animal than human. I had forgotten about her. Lara was standing in the middle of the snow holding a blanket in her shaking hands.

"Kit," she cried out, her voice filled with fear.

"Don't come any further," I said. My teeth were chattering.

Instead of turning away and going back to the house, she came forward, one arm outstretched, her feet sinking into the snow. I pulled Chepi's still warm carcass into my lap and heaved her up as I got onto to my feet.

Carrying the dead body of my daughter, I walked towards Lara.

As we reached Lara, her hand connected with my arm. Instinctively and quickly she threw the blanket over my shoulders. Then we ploughed back to the house through the thick snow where I laid Chepi on the floor of my living room.

My feet were blue and I was shivering uncontrollably.

Lara came close to me and pressed her body to mine. I had been alone for so long. Closed off to everyone. Then this woman came, brought a sweetness I had never known and ... an enemy.

Someone who doesn't want me to be with her.

Thirty-five

Lara

We buried Chepi that morning. The air was still and bitingly cold, and I could hear the wolves milling about. Kit said wolves could smell death from an awful long distance, but I don't know if they completely understood that Chepi was gone forever. They must have known something serious was happening though, because the mood was somber.

Kit cried for her last night.

He left the bed before dawn and quietly crept downstairs to sit with her. When I went down an hour later I crouched down beside him and held his face in my palms. His tears wet my hand. It was as if he lost a child.

"I'm so sorry," I said.

"Her suffering was short," he said quietly.

I never realized just how much he loved that wolf, but I knew how he felt. I had lost the ones I loved before, and I knew that there was not a single thing anyone could say that would have made things better for me. Only time could slowly make you forget the worst of the pain. I just held him tightly in my arms and cried for him.

Now as I stood in the cold, still air, listening to the sound of the earth falling on poor Chepi, I didn't feel sad. I felt fury. I knew exactly who had done this. I couldn't tell Kit because that could escalate everything out of control. Sawyer, being the coward he was, would simply deny everything. Everyone else, except, maybe Elaine, would think I was a fantasist looking for attention.

Who in their right mind would even believe that a handsome man, engaged to the belle of the town, would be so infatuated with a blind girl he would come out in the middle of a freezing night and kill a wolf belonging to her lover? It sounded unbelievable and crazy even to me.

"Come on. Let's go in," Kit said.

I turned towards him, my hands outstretched. "I love you, Kit."

He drew in a ragged breath. "I hope the day never comes that you regret you ever met me."

I frowned. "Why should I regret loving you? You're a good and kind man."

"I hope you'll always remember that," he said sadly.

"What is it, Kit?" I asked worriedly.

He took my hand in his and placed his cold lips lightly on my cheek. "Let's go back inside. You're freezing."

"Are you hiding something from me, Kit?" My voice came out hushed and frightened, even though I was not. Not even a bit. I trusted him with my life.

"For what it's worth, darling, I'd rather die than lie to you, or see harm come to you. Let's not talk of that now. It will all come out one day."

His hand tightened around mine and my insides churned as he began to lead me towards the house.

Thirty-six

Kit

Sheriff Bradley was a man with sly eyes. You could find men like him all over America. Corrupt excuses for men, who were not interested in the truth or upholding the law. They were only interested in being the lapdogs of the richest families in their counties, going to extremes to help them maintain their wealth. In return they get to play a little power trip game called "I'm The Sheriff" for as long as possible.

The Sheriff squinted his eyes at the bloody arrow I had placed on his table. "So no one actually threatened you?" he said. There was something challenging about his voice.

It made my blood boil, but I controlled it. Nothing was going to bring Chepi back, but I needed to send a warning to my enemies. They had fucked with the wrong guy. "No."

"So it could be kids messing about with arrows."

"It could, but it's not. It happened at 3.00 a.m."

"Could be hunters then."

"Wolves are protected by law. No one is allowed to hunt them down ... Sheriff."

His glance flicked at me, then away. "I'll investigate of course, but it'll be hard to find someone based on an arrow. A lot of people have crossbows these days."

I took a step closer and watched his body make an involuntary start in fear. "It belongs to a very expensive weapon. At a guess, I'd say it was a PSE Tac Elite, but since you've got the arrow you don't need me to tell you that. You can track it down easily. And once you find out that it is a $3,000 weapon, I'd start with the grand families of this fine town."

He sucked his teeth. "Like I said, I'll investigate, but I don't hold out much hope. As you're probably aware, crossbow owners are not required to have licenses."

"There are tire and boot marks outside my property."

"I'll get my deputy to go on by and check the evidence." The way he said evidence set my teeth on edge, but there was not a thing I could do about it.

I took a step back. "You be sure to warn all your mighty friends that I don't have very good eyesight, and if I catch anybody prowling around on my land at night, I could mistake him for a bear, shoot first, then ask questions later."

The Sheriff bristled impotently. "Are you threatening to shoot one of the town folk?"

"No, I'm threatening to shoot any bear that comes onto my property."

"Good, because if you cause any trouble in my town I'll haul your ass behind those bars so fast, it'll make your head spin," he said, jerking his head towards a door where his lockup probably was.

The idea of the bloated worthless man hauling my ass off to his jailhouse was laughable. I smiled nastily. “If you don’t like your townspeople shot, I suggest you find my shooter before I find bears on my land.”

Then I turned around and got out of his office.

As I walked across the road to the pickup, I could see Lara’s white face through the windshield. She looked so lost and vulnerable that something inside me broke even more. I’d been lying to her. Soon I’d have to tell her the truth. I just hoped she’d take it better than I expected her to. I took the last few steps, opened the door, and climbed in.

“What did he say?” she asked cautiously. She obviously already knew exactly what the good Sheriff would say.

“He said he’d send his deputy around to look at the tracks, but he made sure I understood that nothing would come of his investigations. In his opinion too many people in this town own crossbows.”

She frowned, then fell strangely quiet.

“What’s the matter?”

“Will you drop me off at the library, Kit. I need to talk to Elaine.”

“I’ll hang around for you.”

“No, I have some chores to do as well. I’ll get Elaine to drop me off at your place later.”

“Nah, the roads are bad. I’ll drive back into town this afternoon for you.”

She nodded, but I could tell her mind was elsewhere. We drove to the library in silence. When I stopped the car, she turned towards me.

Her hand reached out and grabbed mine. She held it tightly. “Take care, darling. Drive safely.”

I got out and helped her get down. A woman in a black coat was watching us. She was frowning. I didn’t give a shit. I wrapped my arms around her and kissed her deeply.

When I raised my face, Lara smiled at me. There was something sad about her smile. “You’re the best thing that ever happened to me, Kit.”

“I hope you’ll always think that.”

She frowned slightly. “Is someone staring daggers at us?”

“Uh huh.”

“It’s a woman in her forties in a black coat and knitted hat, isn’t it?”

I glanced back at the biddy. If looks could kill ... “Bang on target.”

“That’s Marybeth Luther, one of the town’s busybodies. I swear she’ll make me so angry one of these days, I’m gonna tell her to stop judging me because the way to God’s heart is the same as a man’s. On your knees.”

I smiled. I loved this woman. I think I’ve loved her from the time I saw her get out of that blue Toyota. It’s easy for people who have many distractions to scoff at the concept of love at first sight. That must be what happened to me. I took one look at this fresh, young, exciting, innocent, sweet girl and fell like a ton of bricks. Until she came I'd fooled myself into believing I needed no one.

"Tell her anyway," I said softly.

"Okay, you better go. I'll see you later."

"No, I'll wait here until you go into the library."

She shook her head. "I need to do some grocery shopping first. Go on. Let me wave to you."

"I'll see you at my house about three o'clock," she said.

"See you later," I said softly.

I left her by the side of the truck and went back in. I watched her wave until I could no longer see her in my rear view mirror.

Thirty-seven

Lara

I didn't go to the grocery store, and I didn't have any errands to run. I shook my cane out and went back the same way we came, back to the Sheriff's office. The pavement was icy and treacherous so I walked slowly. When I opened the door to his office, he was about to go home. He was standing by the coat rack.

"Lara," he said, his voice lacking any warmth at all.

"Hello Sheriff."

"I was just about to leave for another meeting, but what can I do for you?"

I walked to his desk and sat opposite his empty chair. Sighing audibly, he placed his hat down on the table, and lowered himself into his chair. "Right. Let's hear it."

"The person who shot the wolf was Sawyer Bennet," I said.

The silence that followed was so profound that the expression you could have heard a pin drop became true.

"Sawyer," he repeated incredulously when he got over his deep shock. "He couldn't hurt a fly if it was shitting on his nose."

"He's not what you think he is," I insisted.

"Well, what is he?" he taunted.

"He's hidden. He's angry, and resentful, and devious. Very devious."

"On what basis are you making this very serious allegation?"

I swallowed. "Because he told me he was going to show Kit."

"Show Kit?" he echoed.

"He was going to punish him," I said impatiently. I knew he was being deliberately obtuse. He was trying to make me feel that I was being stupid or irrational.

"Punish him for what?"

"For being with me."

"Why should Sawyer Bennet care who you're with?"

"Because he's in love with me."

Sheriff Bradley coughed politely. "Lara, are you aware that Sawyer is about to feature in the Haverbrooke's family portrait?"

"Yes, but he confessed to me that he's in love with me, and he's just marrying her for the money," I cried. I could see that, just as I had expected, I was getting nowhere. I even sounded completely crazy to my own ears.

The Sheriff cleared his throat. "Look, Lara. I know Sawyer is prettier than a sugar lump, and every unmarried gal this side of the river is secretly sweet on him, but don't you think you're carrying this too far."

"I'm not telling a story," I almost shouted with frustration.

"I'm not calling you a liar, buttercup, but is it possible that you could have misheard, or ... misunderstood?"

"I'm blind, Sheriff Bradley, not stupid."

"It's my job to look out for you, but I won't be able to protect you if you insist on practicing bein' married to Carson, and go around making all kinds of outlandish accusations. Have you told Carson what you just told me?"

"No."

"Good. I suggest you don't. We can't have everyone taking the law into their own hands. He's not proper civilized, that Carson. He's got the makings of a hothead. So you leave it to me. I'll conduct a proper investigation into the matter."

"Will you talk to Sawyer?"

"If I find any evidence to implicate him, I'll do more than talk to him. You can be right sure of that."

"I want you to tell him that if he doesn't stop coming around to Old Man's Creek and causing trouble, I'll call old man Haverbrooke myself."

At the mention of the Haverbrooke name the very air in the room changed, became colder than a frog's behind.

"I wouldn't advise that course of action, Lara. Mr. Haverbrooke is a very busy man, and he doesn't take kindly to unfounded, unproven slurs to his family name."

"Well, I'm not lying," I cried hotly. "You can believe me or not, but I wanted it noted that I came here and told you that Sawyer Bennet is dangerous and needs to be stopped."

"My cat is more dangerous than Sawyer. I don't know where you got the impression that he's dangerous, or in love with you, but he looks like a very happy soon-to-be-groom to me."

"I think you'll find that he owns a crossbow."

"I think you should stop poking about in other people's business." His voice had lost that honeyed cajoling tone and was downright stern.

"I'll lay money that you'll find he was there last night. You'll see his shoe prints and his tire tracks in the snow."

"It's possible he was out hunting around Old Man's Creek, but that's not exactly a crime," he said calmly.

"It's not hunting season," I retorted angrily.

"It's getting late. You better run on home, or back to Carson if that's where you're heading."

I stood up, frustrated, furious, and helpless. "You won't do anything about what I've just told you, will you?"

"I will. As soon as I get some evidence," he said calmly. "I can't go cautioning people on the say-so of a slip of a girl."

I nodded. "Fine. I will take care of this myself."

"Take a bit of fatherly advice from me, young lady. Stay away from Sawyer and his family. Don't think I won't put you behind bars just because you're blind."

"Thank you for your time, Sheriff. You've been most helpful," I said through clenched teeth, and stormed out of his office.

Outside, it was snowing lightly. Light flakes fell on my face. I turned towards the high street. Jimbo, the guy from whom I bought most of my wood pieces for my art, stopped his pickup to ask if I wanted a lift home.

"Thanks," I said, and got into his overly hot truck, with its smell of damp dog, and the sound of windshield wipers swishing.

"You look damn near frozen, girl."

"It's cold," I agreed.

"It's about to turn colder than my mother-in-law's heart tonight," he said.

"Jimbo," I said, "you hunt, don't ya?"

"Sure do."

"Do you ever hunt with Sawyer?"

"Keen shot, he is, but I haven't been out shooting with him ever since he got that corncob stuck up his ass, pardon my French."

"Does he use a gun, Jimbo?"

"We don't nobody use guns no more, lass. Crossbows: they're the business. Fast, quiet, and deadlier than my mother-in-law."

I bit my lip. "Does everybody use crossbows nowadays then?"

"Well, the smart ones do."

So the Sheriff was right when he said a lot of hunters had crossbows.

"Do you know what kind of crossbow Sawyer has?"

"He had the same model as me, but I heard he's upgraded. The lads were saying his sweetheart gave him a real fancy one for his birthday." He wound down the glass and spat into the street.

Thirty-eight

Lara

That night Kit was restless. He kept going out to check on the wolves, and earlier, the whole time he was eating the roast chicken I'd cooked, I could feel how tense he was. He would suddenly go quiet, as if he was listening out for unusual noises.

In bed, we made love, but he was different. He pounded into me as if there were demons driving him. It was the same man, same body, but the drive was different. Later, he apologized, if he had been too rough, if he had hurt me.

"No, you didn't hurt me. I enjoyed it," I told him.

He took me again, this time gently, holding back and letting me climax before he'd allow himself to. I fell asleep in his arms.

I woke up cold. He was not next to me. I pulled on some clothes and went downstairs. He was outside in the freezing cold sitting on the old, tall chair with the wolves gathered around him. I could tell instantly that they were mourning. They seemed to be such a close-knit unit, I almost felt as if I was intruding.

"What are you doing?" I whispered from the doorway.

"I couldn't sleep," he said.

"You'll catch a cold."

I heard him stand up and walk towards me. He touched my face and his hands were like little blocks of ice.

"You're freezing," I said anxiously.

"I'm used to the cold." He wrapped his big arms around me.

I shivered. "Do you want me to make you a cup of hot chocolate? I brought marshmallows."

"Oh, Lara. I don't know what I did to deserve you, but I thank God every day for you."

I smiled up at him. "Is that a yes?"

"That's a yes."

"Sit by the fire and wait for me. I won't be long," I said, but he didn't go in and make himself comfortable by the fire, he followed me into the kitchen and sat at the table.

Into a saucepan I put four tablespoons of cocoa powder, and an equal amount of sugar. "I'll have to go back tomorrow," I said. "I've got to finish my mermaid."

"All right. I'll take you back after breakfast."

"Thank you," I said as I added a pinch of salt, and two tablespoons of milk into the mixture. I put the pan over a low heat and started to whisk it. Listening to the sound the whisk made, I could tell when the sugar was dissolved. I poured the rest of the milk and carried on whisking.

"I'll get the mugs," Kit said.

I poured the creamy hot liquid into the mugs. "Would you prefer marshmallows or a boozy addition?" I asked.

"Boozy?" he said.

I pulled out the bottle of Bourbon from the cupboard and gave it to him. I heard him pour in a generous amount while I tore open the packet of mini marshmallows and dropped a handful into my drink. Then we went into the living room and drank our chocolate by the fire.

"Do you know anyone who is against the idea of you being with me?" he asked suddenly.

"Everybody, I would have thought," I said slowly. I couldn't tell him the truth. As much as I hated to admit it, Sheriff Bradley was right. I could make things a lot worse. I needed to talk to Sawyer myself first.

I felt him shift and lean forward. "No, someone who is angry about it. Someone who feels the need to take revenge. But a coward. A man. A man who feels something for you."

I bent towards my mug so he wouldn't be able to see the expression on my face. "Maybe it is a good idea to let Sheriff Bradley investigate first."

He stood up and paced the floor. "He's not going to do anything, Lara. His job is not to uphold law and order. His real purpose is to protect the rich. He's their attack dog."

"But he can't just not do anything. He has to investigate."

"Yeah, I've seen sham investigations before. I know exactly what his investigations will turn up. Nothing."

"At least give him a chance," I said, and hated the way I sounded even as I made the pathetic suggestion.

"I can't sit here while out there roams a man who can shoot my wolves anytime he pleases. He could be out there right now, Lara. Just waiting for the lights to go off so he can fire another arrow."

I covered my face with my hands. I felt so guilty. If not for me Chepi would not be dead. Even now I couldn't tell him what I knew, because I was afraid he would do something crazy, and end up behind bars. Everybody in this town was just waiting for him to put a foot wrong.

He strode towards me and crouched in front of me. Gently he grasped my hands with his and removed them from my face. "You know something, don't you?"

"I can't tell you yet," I whispered. "Please don't ask me to tell you."

"Are you protecting someone?" he asked in a shocked voice.

"Yes. I'm protecting you," I sobbed.

"Me? It's not your job to protect me, Lara. I'm here to protect you."

"If you approach him it will only make things worse. Let me talk to him first."

"What?" he exploded. "No fucking way. It'll be a cold day in hell before I let my woman be in the same room as a coward who has to make his point with a crossbow from sixty yards away."

"I won't talk to him," I said immediately. "I'll talk to someone he respects. Someone he'll never dare go against."

"Lara, I don't know how your brain works, but no, that is not an acceptable solution. You have to trust me. I'm not a fool. I won't go crazy. I won't hurt anyone, but I need you to tell me so I can sort this out. My wolves are sitting ducks out there while this maniac is allowed to run free."

"It's not so simple."

"No?"

I shake my head.

"Explain it to me." He sounded like he was losing his patience.

"He's in love with me, but he's marrying another woman for her money. He thought no one else would want me, and that in two years he would have made a pile of money using her father's contacts, and then he would be able to divorce her and marry me."

"Fuck, what a sick piece of shit," he spat.

"So you see, I don't want to spoil it for him, because then it will be worse for us. I just want to warn him to stay away because I'm with you and he's with her. I think I can convince him that I love you, and he might as well stick with her as there is no hope for him and me."

"You'll do no such thing. The man is dangerous and-." He broke off mid-sentence and froze. "Someone's coming. Stay here. Don't move," he ordered, and I could hear his footsteps running to get his weapon. Then, to my astonishment, he stopped running, and paused for a second before he started walking back towards me. He stood in front of me, and all the anger and tension had drained out him.

Suddenly, he seemed like a beaten man.

"What?" I whispered, more frightened than I had ever been in my life.

He knelt beside me, and I reached out a trembling hand to touch his face. His eyes were closed with regret or sorrow. I could hear a vehicle coming up the road.

“Who is coming?” I asked, my voice shaking

“Oh, Lara. I never meant for you to find out like this.”

Thirty-nine

Lara

https://www.youtube.com/watch?v=L3wKzyIN1yk

"Find out what?" I gasped.

He sagged, his forehead rested against my chest, and the feeling that something was not just wrong, but horribly wrong descended on me like a sheet thrown over a bed. It was not heavy enough to take my breath, but light enough to give me goosebumps. I sat there like a statue, my hands gripping the table edge, the now-familiar whisper of the fire in the woodstove loud in the strange silence.

Then came the sound of men's voices. They stopped outside. They were waiting. But for what? Kit? Who were they and why was he not going outside?

I touched his face. "What's going on Kit?" I begged, there was more than an edge of panic in my voice.

"I have to go," he said.

"Go? Go where?"

"I can't leave you here on your own, not with that sorry son of a bitch running loose, so I'm going to take you back to your house."

“Kit, first tell me what the heck is going on? You’re scaring me. Who are those men outside?”

There was a firm knock on the front door.

“I’ll explain it all when I get back in two, maximum three days.”

I grabbed his shirt. “No, I can’t wait. You have to tell me now.”

The knocking got louder. “Kit,” someone called.

“Let me go answer that fucking door,” he said.

I let go of his shirt and tuned out everything but what was going on at the front door. The door swung open on its well-oiled hinges, and the man spoke in a low voice. I strained to catch what he was saying, but I couldn’t make anything out. I stood up and walked to the corridor.

“Take her to her house? What the fuck? She’ll see us, man!”

“She’s blind,” Kit said.

“How far away is the town?”

“Half an hour.”

“Can’t you just leave her here?”

“No fucking way. You have three choices. I take her home and meet you back here, we drop her off and go on from there, or I don’t come at all.”

The man sighed. “I’ll have to call it in, but I guess it’ll be easier if we drop her off.”

The door closed. I heard the man walk away. Then I heard Kit run up the stairs, taking them two, or three at a time.

In a confused daze, I stood up and walked to the living room. Unthinkingly, I sat on the armchair by the fire. The spring jagged into my flesh and I remembered that first morning I came here. How much my life had changed since then. My heart was racing and my mind was trying to figure out what the conversation with the man had been about. Who was that man? Where were they going? Why did it matter that I did not see them?

Whatever it was, I was going to be dropped off home. I stood up and walked towards the stairs. I went upstairs to the bedroom.

"Get dressed," he said. "We'll drop you off at your house."

It was Kit, but it wasn't my Kit ... not exactly. This man had the gruff edge, the steel-hard undertone that I had heard when he spoke to me on the telephone that first time. This was what everybody else got. Not me. He'd never been like this with me.

I stood there in a state of shock. He was like a stranger. I wanted to cry. His steps came toward me.

He was wearing heavy boots, different than his usual ones. He even smelled different, a blend of sandalwood, and metal and something else, something I couldn't put my finger on. His clothing rustled in a way that I hadn't heard before. The moment he was close enough I reached out to touch him.

The fabric was rough. My hand went over his heart, to my favorite place in this world, and there was an even rougher spot. A patch? I dug my nails into it. It pulled off with the ripping sound of Velcro.

“What’s going on, Kit?” My heart was pounding so hard that I could feel it from head to toe.

“Honey, get ready. Please,” he said, his voice full of regret.

“What is this?” I demanded, holding out the patch. “Is this a name tag?”

Kit paused. “Yes.”

“Are you in uniform?”

“Yes.”

“Why are you in uniform?” I was genuinely confused. He had never mentioned a uniform, never said anything about it. If his voice hadn’t held that edge … if there hadn’t been such regret in it now … maybe I could have believed he was wearing it for old time’s sake.

But he wasn’t, and I knew it.

“Sit down for a minute,” he said, taking my free hand, and pulling me toward the bed. I went willingly, sinking down onto the crisply folded blankets and perfectly tucked sheets. My brain processed that information. He’d made the beds. What the hell? Why would he do that if he was in a hurry? Was it for the same reason that people worry about having clean underwear if they met with an accident? My mind went blank.

“What is going on?” I sat there, clutching his hand, willing myself to hear everything, even the things he couldn’t, or wouldn’t say. I was scared, and I didn’t know why.

Kit sighed. “I was going to explain all of this to you, but the time was never right,” he said. “After what you told me about your brother and your dad, I realized that I might have waited too long already. Then we just kept getting closer, and closer and I didn't want to spoil that." He cleared his throat. "I knew telling you would spoil it."

"Spell this out for me, Kit," I whispered. "The suspense is killing me."

He paused for a long moment. When he next spoke, his voice was thick with tears. "I'm in uniform because I'm a covert operative, Lara," he said.

I couldn't breathe. The air wouldn't come. I stood up, and the motion somehow jolted my body into doing what it should do. I took a deep breath as the disbelief set in.

I sat back down like a robot. "Say that again." I hoped I had heard him wrong.

"I'm what is known in the business, Lara, as sheep dipped."

Forty

Lara

"Sheep dipped?" I repeated. I actually felt dizzy with confusion. My life felt like it had been turned upside down. "For Pete's sake, Kit, stop talking in damn riddles. What the heck is sheep dipped?" I lashed out.

"It's someone who gives every impression of being a civilian, or one of the sheep, but in fact, is in deep cover. We carry out the operations that our government does in secret."

"You can't be," I gasped. I ran both my hands through my hair. My whole life was turning out to be a bizarre, unbelievable nightmare. First, Sawyer told me he was secretly in love with me, then the man that Sheriff Bradley said wouldn't kill a fly that was shitting on his face came around and killed an innocent wolf, now Kit was telling me he was some sort of black operative in the military.

How could this have happened to me? I didn't even want a soldier, and I get a Delta Force, or Navy SEALs, or whatever the hell his squad was called.

"I am, Lara. That's what I do. I'm part of a special forces team. I was recruited into it seven years ago. Me and my battle buddies were chosen because of our skill sets, our lack of family, our mental make-up, and our dedication to our units. Whenever a job comes up that our government cannot be seen to be involved in, they come and get me."

"A job?" I whispered.

"They are jobs. In and out, short and sweet, one and done. When they are done, I come back here and become the guy who was discharged from the army and is suffering from a mild form of PTSD again ..."

I felt sick to the core. "This has to be a joke."

His voice was filled with regret. "I wish it were."

"You said you used to be in the military. Not that you were neck deep in it!" I accused.

"I never said that. I never said I was done. I would never do that, because that would be lying ... to you, my angel."

"And lying by *omission* is okay?" I screeched.

My voice was so loud it echoed around the room. I couldn't breathe properly. I wanted to lay down on his bed, crawl into a fetal position, and cry until there was no pain left and the awful thoughts going through my head were dead. But I was stronger than that. Wasn't I?

"Fine, tell me everything now then. I want to know," I demanded. The voice that came out of me was so intense as to be almost foreign.

"I can't tell you anything. You shouldn't even know what you already do. We're not even allowed to reveal our true status to anyone, not even our families. For most part the families of black operatives think their loved ones are either discharged because of injury, sickness or mental problems."

"Am I allowed to know where you are going tonight?"

"I don't know yet. I'll be briefed once I get to the base."

"What will you be doing?"

"Even if I knew, I couldn't tell you."

"But they are all dangerous assignments?"

"Some are more dangerous than others."

"Oh my God! You could die tonight, couldn't you?" I gasped.

"Yes." The word was spoken quietly, but it hit my heart like a bullet.

"I can't believe this. No way. This is not happening to me again. You're calmly telling me you could walk out of that door and never come back! Like my brother and my father." My voice was shrill with the hysteria of thinking he could die.

"What does black ops mean? Are you doing illegal things?"

"Often, that is the reason we are used."

"Why?"

"Because the end justifies the means."

"If you're doing illegal things it means what you are doing is wrong."

"There is a big difference between what is legal and what is morally right and wrong. What is legal changes with time. Once it was legal to hunt wolves. Now it isn't. Once it was legal to buy and sell black people. Now it isn't. I'm doing the right thing. Someone has to stop the horrible things that happen in this world. Someone has to step up and do the right thing."

By then I was crying, but my voice was steady. "Why does that someone have to be you?"

"If everybody thought that about their loved ones then there would be no one left to step up to the job."

"I have given up my dad, my brother, and my mother for my country. Are you asking me to give up the man I love for this country as well?"

"Can we talk about this when I get back?"

"What is there to talk about?" I asked bitterly. "Not only are you a soldier, you're part of a unit that undertakes the most dangerous missions." I stopped. "Do you kill people in these secret missions?"

"Sometimes."

I covered my mouth with my hands. "Who are you?"

"I'm the man who never thought he'd find a woman again. I'm the guy who'd given up hope. I'm the man who loves you."

If he had said those words a few hours back I would have been the happiest woman on earth, but now, they rung hollow. Love? This was not love. He tricked me. He knew I never wanted to be with a man in the army and he let me fall in love with him. "If something happens to you this time, and you don't come back, will I even know about it?"

The silence was like a knife in my chest.

"I won't even be told, will I?" I croaked in disbelief.

"Probably not. You'll just read in the paper that a veteran died in an automobile crash on one of the roads nearby, or something like that."

Forty-one

Lara

I shook my head in astonishment. "Oh, Jesus! Can you hear yourself? Do you even understand what you're asking of me?"

He didn't reply and I wanted to shake him with frustration and rage.

"What if it was me? What if it was me being called out in the middle of the night, and there was a better-than-great chance that you'd never see me again?"

I heard him take a shuddering breath.

"Answer me!" I shouted.

"No, I wouldn't allow you to go."

"So how can you ask that of me?" I cried.

"There is a big difference between us. I'm not a novice. I'm a highly trained soldier. There are not many men who are better at what I do than me. I'm good at this, Lara. It's why I was recruited."

"Is that why you nearly got blown to smithereens before?"

He sighed heavily. "If I am meant to die, Lara, I will. I could slip in the snow and fall while I'm carrying you to our front door and go that way."

"Is that meant to be your idea of a joke?" I gasped.

"I have to go now, but I'll be back in three days. Please don't try to contact that sorry son of a bitch until I return."

I nodded automatically and heard the clink of something, an out of context sound, but one that I had heard before. Then it finally registered – that smell I couldn't put my finger on, that strangely familiar scent. It was gun oil. Suddenly, I knew. I took a deep breath. It hurt me to my very core.

"I promised myself I would never go through what my mother went through," I said. "I didn't tell you what happened after my father's funeral, did I? My mother held it together through all of that, through the damn flag folding, and the salute; and all the fine-standing men in uniform saying they were so sorry. She made it back home and smiled bravely at the reception, but when everyone was gone, she collapsed on the floor in her bedroom and screamed. She screamed, and screamed, and ... I ... I ... couldn't make her stop." My voice had risen to a hysterical pitch.

"Don't. Don't, Lara. Don't do this," he begged, holding me tightly.

I was crying so hard I could barely breathe. "She was never the same after that. Never. I won't go down that path. I can't. I don't want to. Please don't ask me to."

"Lara, let us talk about this, please. I want to explain it to you so that you can understand that-"

"No," I snarled at him suddenly. Pulling out of his grasp I stood. "You want me to understand? You mean you want me to condone your the-ends-justifies-the-means philosophy and pardon your lies."

"I never lied to you. You assumed because I lived alone in the middle of nowhere, and didn't seem to get posted that I was no longer in the army."

"If I had known this is what you did I never would have spent that night here during the storm. I never would have done the things we did," I cried passionately.

Kit stood up and took a step towards me. He was so close I could feel the heat and tension coming off his body.

"Lara, why do you think I pushed you away that first night? It is because of what you told me about your father and brother. But you came to me again in the night, and I wasn't strong enough to push you away. How could I? You were everything I ever dreamed of, ever wanted."

"You said I might regret sleeping with you," I said to him, my voice harsh and bitter. "Well, you were right. I do regret it. With all my heart." I vomited those words deliberately, to wound, and it seemed I succeeded.

Kit sucked in a breath and froze, as if I had shot him.

Because my heart was hurting, because I wanted to curl my hands around his neck and beg him not to go. I turned and started to walk away, but going a bit faster than I should have, I bumped into the corner of a side table, stumbled, and would have fallen if Kit had not grabbed me.

"Lara ..."

"No, don't touch me," I screamed. "You're worried about me getting a little knock while you're merrily ripping my heart to shreds."

He let go of me as if I was fire. Holding myself stiffly, I began to make my way to where my clothes were. Kit was right behind me. "Lara, please ... I know this looks bad, and I am so sorry I didn't tell you, but please give us a chance."

My tears were suddenly dry. I turned on him slowly. He didn't sound sorry at all. It was simply another facet of his the-ends-justifies-the-mean strategy. "I don't know where you're going. I don't know what you will be doing. And I can't live like that."

"I will be back in three days," he said. "And then we can talk."

His voice was so plaintive and in normal circumstances I would have given in, but I thought about the neighbors banging on the door and my mother screaming until she fainted. Through all of this I had kept his name tag in my clenched fist. I took a deep breath and placed my other hand on his chest. Finding the Velcro there, I stuck his name tag on it.

"Be careful," I said softly. "Even though you are not for me I don't want anything to happen to you."

He didn't try to stop me when I took a step back and went to the chair where I had put my clothes.

"Lara," he begun, finally.

I whirled on him. "Enough. Please. You lied. You lied to me about something that you knew was so important to me. I thought I was part of something special with you and the wolves. How can I ever trust you again?"

I could hear him swallow from where I stood. Turning away from him I pulled my jeans on, and quickly grabbed my top. My hands fumbled for my sweater. It was not on the chair where I put it. I heard him walk towards me. He picked it off the floor where it had fallen, and thrust it into my hand.

I wanted to cry, but I choked it down, took my sweater out of his hand, and pulled it roughly over my head. Then I walked out of the room and down the stairs with him following me. I went to the hallway, and taking my coat off the hook on the wall, put it on. While I buttoned up and got my hat and my scarf on, he went around switching things off. The house fell silent until only the sound of his boots echoed through the house.

I didn't want to talk to him anymore so I opened the door and stepped out on the porch. As Jimbo had predicted it was a freezing cold night. All the wolves had disappeared. Kit once told me that the wolves lived in the forest whenever he went away and only returned to the house when he came back.

I could feel the men in the car watching me. The ground was slippery with black ice so I waited for him to close the door. Silently, I let him take my hand and help me down the steps. Kit opened the back door and I climbed in.

There were two men in the car, but nobody said anything until Kit climbed in next to me.

"This is Lara, guys. Lara, the driver is Jerry, and the asshole sitting next to him is Billy." He tried to pretend that nothing was wrong, but his voice was completely off key.

"Thanks a bunch, dude. Hey, Lara," Billy said good-naturedly.

"How's it going, Lara?" Jerry asked.

"Fine, thank you," I whispered.

The car began to move. I sat in a daze as we covered the miles. I wanted to cry so badly, but I gritted my teeth and forced myself to sit straight and as far away as I could from Kit.

As we got into town, Kit began to give instructions. The car came to a stop on the street outside my house. I heard Kit's door open, and blindly I turned towards my door handle. I didn't want him to help me. I opened the door, and my foot sunk into snow. Kit was already there, and he took my hand.

"I can manage from now on. You can go," I told him coldly.

"No, I'll walk you to your door."

"That won't be necessary. Thank you."

"Fuck it, Lara. I'm either helping you to your door or I'm carrying you to it. Make your choice."

I swallowed. I didn't even know which way to turn, which just made me feel sad and unhappy. I put my hand on his arm. Instantly, the hard muscles underneath tensed. He exhaled, and for a second I thought he was going to say something, but he just took a step forward. At my door, he waited for me to put the key in and open it.

"Goodnight, my love. I'll be thinking of you," he whispered.

I couldn't help it then, a tear slipped out.

He reached out a hand and wiped it away. "I love you," he said, "so much it hurts."

"Then don't go," I cried.

"It's my job, Lara."

"Get another job," I pleaded.

"It's what I'm best at. I don't know how to do anything else."

"I've got enough money saved. We'll live off my art." Tears were running quickly down my cheeks.

"We'll talk about it when I come home."

"There's nothing to talk about. You're either with me, or in the military."

He bent his head and gently kissed my forehead. Then he was gone. I went into my house, closed the door, and listened to the car door slam, the engine start, and the car drive off into the night.

Then, I walked to my kitchen. My steps were a little wobbly, but I was all right. I switched on the heater. I walked to the kettle and filled it. Still in my coat I made myself a mug of tea.

Then, I went into the living room. The house was still very cold so I switched on the little two bar heater that I kept for emergencies. I sat down near it. The heat warmed my feet.

I touched the face of my watch. Three thirty-five. I should go to bed, but I wasn't sleepy. I took a sip of tea and tasted nothing.

At that moment I felt there was no one in Durango Falls, or the world, who felt more alone and abandoned than me. I finished my tea and went upstairs. My steps were slow, like those of an old woman. I didn't allow myself to cry. I had plenty of time for that.

I knew I would be crying for years to come.

Forty-two

Kit

https://www.youtube.com/watch?v=vt1Pwfnh5pc

Call me a son of a bitch for not telling her the truth from the start, call me shit for brains, call me anything, but I'm not sorry. I love that woman too much to give a flying fuck about fair play or what anyone else thinks. Even if the rules I was sworn to uphold allowed me to tell her what I was involved in, which by the fucking way it didn't, I was not about to lose the one thing in my life that was pure and perfect.

So, yeah, I'm a selfish prick, but news flash, I never claimed to be a saint, and if I had to do it all again, I'd do the same fucking thing. Why would I take even the smallest risk of her walking away? This way I got through her first line of defense, and won myself a chance to fight another day. Whatever happens now, she loves me and it'll be that much harder for her to keep resisting me. I'll fight for her until she breaks down and takes me back, or I'll be camped outside her front door because I ain't no quitter.

I forced myself to stop thinking about Lara. I shouldn't. Not if I wanted to get out of this alive. My focus had to be on survival. For me and the eight guys who came on this assignment with me. One small mistake and I was never seeing that angel face, or tasting her sweet flesh again.

I was lying down on a bed of wet leaves in the middle of a Columbian jungle wearing night vision goggles and black fatigues with no insignia. Anything goes wrong and I get discovered, there would be no blow back. We were men who didn't exist.

Something slimy crawled onto my hand. Oh fuck. That's all I need, another leech. I can't light a cigarette here, so I'm gonna have to let it feast until this scenario is over. I squinted my eyes and looked down the sight of my sniper gun.

I was looking at a big ole warehouse painted green to blend with the jungle. It was protected by a tall electric fence and, at last count, eight security guards trained to kill. Probably hired guns, mercenaries. Inside the warehouse was the biggest cache of illegal weapons and high grade cocaine. One day I would make Lara understand.

Someone has to do this.

If we didn't take care of this tonight, tomorrow morning a long convoy of trucks would appear at the gates of the warehouse. One at a time, the vehicles would back up to the building, and men would forklift out boxes upon boxes of cheap television sets stuffed full of cocaine. They would fill up one truck after another, then the trucks would be off to a port, where money would grease hands, men with families would look the other way.

The shipment would land in my country where hordes of people would maim, steal, and kill for it. That's what was supposed to happen tomorrow, but tonight, I was here, and what was going to happen just became a whole different story.

My team and I were the difference.

A black 4x4 drove up, the headlights cutting through the dark. The guards rushed to open the metal gates. The vehicle stopped in front of the warehouse door. I shifted my attention to the vehicle door closest to the entrance. A man's dark head emerged, then his body and one of his legs followed. I trained my crosshairs on an imaginary orange dot on his back.

The instant kill shot.

In a few days, I would think about him again. I would be halfway through a bottle of whiskey, and I would wonder why there were so many like him. How had humanity come to a place where it was men like him who had all the money and ruled over the rest of us?

But deep thoughts and covert activities were like work boots on a poodle. They didn't mix. Tonight, I wouldn't consider anything more than the straightforward fact: he was standing between me and my objective.

The voice in my earpiece whispered, "We're a go."

Before his other leg could touch the ground, I pulled the trigger.

The man sagged and fell out of the 4x4. My shot was true; he was done before his head hit the ground. A man rushed out of the front passenger's seat. I had him before he could get to the door of the warehouse. There was shouting and screaming. The car began to reverse with a panicked screech.

I pulled the trigger again.

The wheels began spinning. Armed men came rushing out of the warehouse. Their deaths came from the other side of the building. That was my buddy, Roger, with his sarcastic smile and his perfect aim. I counted eight.

The sudden peal of an ear-piercing siren caught me off guard. "Shit!"

Lights facing out into the jungle went on around the entire compound, lighting up the night as if it were day. I blinked.

Ah, not the first time. Wrong intel. Our careful plan had just gone to hell in a damp jungle. Now we were in the thick of it, well before we had intended to be. Still, the momentum was on our side. I watched the warehouse for any signs of life.

There was the glint of a rifle from an upstairs window.

I aimed and fired. The first bullet chipped through the stucco. The second bullet shattered the window, and whoever was in there screamed loudly enough for me to hear him. A bullet came flying my way, thudding into the soft ground two feet away from me. That was too close for comfort.

Here we go, champ. Let's play.

I rose up and started a quick trek along the ridge, running hard. He was still trying. I could hear the whoosh and thump as the bullets missed their mark. He wasn't leading, which told me he wasn't a sniper. He was just somebody who almost got lucky.

I knelt behind a tree and waited. I was at the right angle to see him make the stupid, rookie mistake that they all make. Only this time, he wouldn't be lucky enough to get out of it alive.

There was the glint of his gun. I waited. There was his hand, clear in my sights. Still, I waited. Then his head came forward, and he put himself in the line of fire in order to see where I was. It was nothing more than a second, but hey, that's all a decorated sniper needs, my friend.

My weapon kicked in my hands, what was left of the window shattered, and upstairs guy was toast.

And that's when all hell broke loose.

Hidden trapdoors all around the compound opened and shots rang out. Apparently, there was far more security than our intelligence had shown – and now that the shit had hit the fan, there was nothing to do but fucking get splattered. Rifle fire followed me down as I threw myself from the cliff onto the ground twelve feet below.

I rolled at the landing to save my knees. I might be a badass, but that didn't mean I was not getting old. At thirty-two I was no spring chicken. I didn't have time to survey the lay of the land. I was being hunted. Covered by the friendly fire, I shouldered my rifle, pulled my sidearm, and headed toward the back of the warehouse.

I blew the lock on the door and slammed it open, surprised that it went so easily, and started my way up the back hallway.

Roger's voice was crystal clear through my earpiece:

"Breached three o'clock, two friendlies."

A man in a suit swung around the corner and raised his gun. His shot went wide, into the wall. Mine went into his chest, and he stumbled back. The bastard was wearing a vest. My second shot went into his head. It exploded backwards like a watermelon.

"They're armored," I said into my radio.

"No shit," came the reply, along with the sound of distant gunfire.

I have always hated close quarter ops, because there isn't any time to think. The second it takes you to decide what to do, is the second the other guy takes you out.

I worked my way through the back rooms. There were more guards than we expected, there weren't nearly enough to stop us. Our guns were silent. I listened as the gunfire slowed down, then ceased completely. I quickly surprised and dispatched two more guys as I cleared my way through to the basement.

The basement opened out onto the hill. There was a large landing pad painted green on the hill. It was empty right now, and there was probably no helicopter coming. Not now that our presence had been revealed way before the operation had a chance to really start. So we might not have got the main guys, but we got the shipment.

Oh, yes.

I stared for a moment at the boxes of guns. They formed a wall across the entire basement. It was a lot more than we had anticipated. How many were there? Well over a thousand, at least. Our job would be over when we torched everything and watched the inferno as we flew away.

Roger came into the room, clearing as he went. He saw me and relaxed. His low whistle cut through the silence when he saw the cache of weapons. He pointed to some boxes at one corner.

"Holy Fuck," he breathed.

I looked. Holy fuck indeed: rocket launchers!

The surprise of it knocked us off our game, just for a split second, but that was all it took.

The shot came from behind Roger. I didn't see the shooter, only his eyes bugging and the sudden gush of blood from his neck as he clutched it, and fell to the floor. I turned in the direction of the fire, and unloaded what I had left in my sidearm, switching to the rifle as I moved behind some boxes. A man dropped with a grunt, his gun clattering to the floor. Rage surged through me and I didn't think as I buried seven shots into his prone body. He was gone to wherever he came from.

But Roger was on his way out too.

"Goddamn it! Medic, we need medical here," I hollered, praying they would get here in time, knowing there was no way they would. I fell to my knees in the blood that was already spreading across the concrete and pulled Roger onto my lap. He looked up at me with those big, brown eyes with their sweep of lush eyelashes. We used to laugh at him. At his girl's eyes. They were filling up with tears now.

"Motherfucker got me," he gasped.

I put my hand on his neck to stem the bleeding. It helped a little, but not half enough. There was no way to save him.

"Roger," I said, "Just hang on."

He grabbed my arm. "Shut up and fucking listen," he whispered, his voice already going.

I shook my head. "The medics are on their way."

"I'm gone, man. I ain't stupid." He started to choke on his own blood.

I lifted his head. "Don't talk," I ordered.

"Listen to me," he rasped, his hands grasping at my shirt. "It's time to get out. We always said we would retire together, remember?"

Roger's eyes filled with tears. "So we're going to. We're going to keep that promise, you fucking hear me, man? I'm leaving the service today. Right now. And when you're done here, you are going to hang up those boots and that gun and you're going home to live your life, man. We're doing this together."

"You're not checking out," I said, holding my hand against his neck, and watching the blood seep out, pooling underneath his head.

He took a breath that rattled in his throat. "It's the beauty of wet work. One day you become it. Promise you won't die like me. Like a fucking dog. There's a reason those fraudulent cocksuckers don't send their own sons to do this work. Promise me!"

By now the tears were running down my face, too.

It's my dying wish," he insisted.

I swallowed the stone in my throat. "Okay, Roger, I promise."

He smiled and coughed. Fuck, a whole cup of blood. It went all over my arm and clothes.

"You deserve something good and sweet, man. You deserve to have a little something for yourself. Remember ... remember when we used to say we wanted to retire to a beach ... and drink beer and hit on girls half our age?"

I nodded.

"Today's the day, my friend. The beer will be so cold it'll fucking hurt, and the sun will always shine, and the women will always think I'm way sexier than you."

I took a deep breath and watched his eyes drift closed. "I've got a woman," I whispered.

His eyes opened slowly. "No shit?" he asked faintly.

"She's beautiful."

Roger gave me the sweetest smile. "You give her a kiss and drink a beer for me."

"I will."

"Tell Marla the truth. She deserves to know why I did what I did."

"I will," I promised.

"Yeah, I should have told her. Tell her I love her."

He closed his eyes.

"You can't sugarcoat shit, man," he whispered, his hands letting go of my shirt.

There was no fanfare. There was just one more breath, and then a silence that stretched on too long ... far too long. And just like that, my best friend was gone.

Forty-three

Lara

"I've always thought you were a bit soft in the head," Elaine said.

"Thanks," I replied.

"No, I'm serious."

"You're not funny, Elaine."

"I wasn't trying to be funny."

"I'm soft in the head simply because I've just changed my mind about Kit?" No, I didn't tell her about the black ops stuff because, of course, it was a secret and Elaine, bless her heart, was not someone you told your secrets to since it would cause her incredible pain to keep it to herself, and why would I want to do that to her when I loved her?

"Not because you've changed your mind, but because the reason you've given me for breaking up is just pathetic. Is it shark week?"

I sighed. "No, it's not that time of the month."

"Then what?" she pressed.

"What's so pathetic about a couple who realize that they are apples and oranges? We both want different things," I said, and hoped she'd be sensitive enough to stop prying anymore. I was already very sad and I wasn't in the mood for a thorough interrogation session with Elaine.

She didn't buy my excuse for a second. "You were in love with him a day ago!" she shot back immediately.

"Well, I've changed my mind."

"Well, I don't believe you."

"Well, that's fine by me. Now can we just drop it?"

"No, I'm not dropping it. This is important. You could be making the biggest mistake of your life."

"It was just a little fling, Elaine. It didn't mean anything."

"Bullcaca! That makes about as much sense as tits on a tree! Stop lying. It's me, Elaine, your best friend from the time we were walking around with diapers full of poo."

I leaned my head against my hand. Honestly, I was dying to tell her everything and cry on her shoulder, but I couldn't. I couldn't betray Kit's secret.

"Did you argue?" she probed.

"Nope."

"Really?" Her voice was disbelieving.

"Maybe a small one."

"What about?"

"He wanted me to do something that I didn't want to."

She drew in a sharp breath. "It was sexual?"

"My God, Elaine. Will you give it a break?"

"So it was sexual!"

I shook my head in exasperation. Maybe I should make something up that would satisfy her. Otherwise, I'd never hear the end of this. I tried to conjure up some perverted thing, but my mind was blank and numb.

"You might as well tell me. I am your best friend in the whole world. Besides, a trouble shared is a trouble halved."

"Stop nagging, Elaine."

"Fine, I got it. I'll stop nagging if you tell me where he is now."

"He's gone to see some friends."

"Is he coming back?"

"I thought you were going to stop."

"I am. Just answer this one last question."

"He'll be back in two days."

"Lara, I know you don't want to talk about this, but as your best friend I have to put it on record that I think you are making a huge mistake. First of all, he made you happy. Ever since you met him you have been walking around like a possum that has stolen into somebody's sweet potato patch. If you could see yourself now. You are trying to pretend you don't care, but your little heart is breaking."

"It's true, I am sad," I confessed, "but it's for the best."

"Most things can be worked out with a little give and take," she said.

I shook my head sadly. "Not this one. Our differences are irreconcilable."

"You know what's irreconcilable. When one party cheats, or beats you up, or doesn't love you back. Everything else is workable. Is it any of the above?"

I shook my head silently.

"Then you owe it to yourself and him to work it out. True love doesn't grow on trees. Do you think something this wonderful will come again in this deadbeat town? Trust me when I say it won't. Even Picket Fence Peter is already taken."

I felt a stab of pain at her words because I knew they were true. No one was ever again going to make me feel the way Kit did or love me the way he did.

"I never interfere in your-"

My head jerked at that statement.

"Okay, I interfere in your life all the time, but hell, I never insist that you listen to me."

I jerked my head meaningfully again.

"Fine, I do insist a lot, but I have never insisted this much before. If you don't try to work this out, you'll regret it for the rest of your life."

My expression must have given me away because she really went for it then.

"Let me ask you something. If you found out that Kit had just one day left to live, would you still insist on fighting with him, or would you make the most of the time left to you?"

I froze. Without knowing it Elaine had hit the nail on the head. What the hell was I doing? I loved Kit with all my heart. In the way that mere words could not describe. Ever since he left last night my heart had turned to stone. The simple truth was my convictions were all well and good in theory, but now that I had gone and fallen head over heels in love with him. I couldn't just walk away and move on. My life belonged with Kit. If I had one day left with him, then I would take that one day. If I had one hour left, I would take that one hour.

I leaned forward and kissed Elaine on the cheek. “Thank God for you, Elaine. You are right. I was being silly about something that can be worked out.”

She clapped her hands with satisfaction. “Good. Put it right as soon as you can.”

“Elaine, if there is absolutely nobody left in this town worth having, who will you end up with?”

“I’m leaving Durango Falls, Lara. I’m not going to rot here. I’m saving up. One of these days I’ll have enough to buy myself a bus ticket to a big bad city.”

“A city? Where?” I gasped.

“Hollywood.”

My mouth dropped open. “You’re thinking of moving to Hollywood!”

“Sure, I am.”

“What will you do there?”

“I don’t know. I’ve been writing little screenplays about life in a small town. I’ll see if I can sell my work, but of course, I’ll start off by waitressing.”

“If you need money, I have some saved up.”

“Nah, I’m still picking up the guts, girding my loins and stuff. You know how it is with Hollywood being full of bitches just waiting to scratch your eyes out. Anyway, we’re not talking about me. We’re talking about you.”

I smiled. “Will you give me a lift to Kit’s house tomorrow? I want to surprise him when he comes back.”

Forty-four

Lara

https://www.youtube.com/watch?v=SBmAPYkPeYU

When we arrived at Kit's house, it was nearly five in the evening. I had learned the shapes and locations of everything inside Kit's house. In fact, I would even go so far as to say I knew it almost as well as I knew my own home. I could glide through the rooms without stubbing a toe or knocking anything off a shelf.

However, I didn't know where the switch for the wood stove was so Elaine came in with me and helped me find it. We didn't light the fire, because neither she nor I knew how to build one that could last more than a few minutes. We had a cup of tea together, but she didn't stay for long because she wanted to get home before dinnertime.

After she had gone I opened Kit's cupboard. All the items in it had been arranged in a specific order so I knew where everything was. I selected a can of tomato soup. While I was pouring it into a saucepan I heard the familiar scratching on the back door. The wolves had sensed that somebody was back. With a happy smile, I opened the door and Lobo and Koa were waiting to greet me. Koa moved away after I gave them a bit of dried meat from the pantry, but Lobo stayed on for more hugs and cuddles. I know Kit said to keep a respectful distance from the wolves as they were not pets, but I completely ignored his instructions and kissed and cuddled Lobo and let him climb all over me.

When he had enough of being manhandled he wandered off and I returned to the kitchen. I warmed the soup, crumbled some cheese into it, and sat down at the table with a hunk of buttered bread.

I could hear the cold wind blowing through the trees, but it was lovely and warm beside the wood stove. I had never been in the house on my own, and it was a strange sensation. I started to think of Kit and my life with him. Would this be what I was consigning myself to?

Long, lonely nights waiting for him to come back. Not sure if he would. What would I do if he didn't? The thought made me feel queasy and I quickly pushed it away and picked up my spoon determined to be positive, but my appetite was gone.

I washed up, put on my parka, hat, and gloves, and grabbing a heavy quilt went outside. The wolves were all back. I could feel and hear them. They came up to the porch to say hello. I sat on the tall chair he sat on and waited.

I was waiting for the sound of the car the men who had come to collect him the other night drove. I was not the only one. My ears might have been more attuned than other sighted humans, but they were nothing like the ears of those wolves.

Three of them joined me on the porch, their noses all turned toward the driveway, their tails flicking against the porch floorboards. Occasionally, one would reach forward and lick my hand. Now and again they would emit the tiniest whines, little worried sounds that made fear crawl up my spine.

I understood that they were waiting for him, too. How many times had they done this? How many times would I have to wait with my heart in my mouth?

I felt my watch face. It was only eight o'clock. Kit said he would be back at the very latest, tonight. I wondered what time he would come back. A thought occurred to me. What if he didn't come back tonight though? What if he never came back?

The more time passed the more I began to regret my actions that night. Even though I had been so damn certain I was done with him, I shouldn't have let him go to his dangerous mission after such a horrible argument. It could have affected his concentration and focus. It was a stupid thing to let him leave on such a bitter note.

I wasn't thinking. All I could hear was the echo of my mother screaming hysterically, and all I could feel was the memory of the sun's rays beating down on my head as I slid my hands over the polished casket. Losing my father was the worst day of my life–right up until the day I lost my brother.

All I could think of was that Kit lied to me, deliberately hid his secret from me. I was furious with him for letting the charade go on even after he knew I had fallen in love with him, but I think what hurt the most was that he was prepared to walk away and go to his job when he could see that I was devastated. It felt as if he chose his job over me.

Ma used to say “happiness is just sadness biding its time”. Maybe I needed to be more patient. Maybe the day will come when he will love me more than his job. He can’t be a soldier forever. Maybe I’ll get luckier than Ma.

Bundled up in a parka and a quilt, and surrounded by an army of wolves, I was snug as a bug in a rug as I waited patiently. An hour passed. Several times I heard cars on the main road, but they did not have the same engine, and sure enough they did not come down the driveway.

Another wolf came onto the porch. I listened to its careful footsteps. They came right up to me, and that big wild animal sat down on his haunches. I felt his breath on my hand, and then his nose bumped my leg. He laid his head on my lap. I touched his muzzle and felt the scars.

Old Andak! Kit’s old, blind buddy. He had come to find me. I had no idea why he would seek me out that night–I will never in a million years understand why–but that was what it took to break me.

Make no mistake: I was one hell of a strong woman. I could handle anything, could take it all on my shoulders and deal with it, but something about that lovely kindred spirit coming to comfort me just did me in.

I leaned forward and buried my face in his thick, warm fur. He leaned into me as I let out a cry that made me sound like a wounded animal myself. It was filled with everything I had held back and fought through these long days and nights–all the worry and pain and fear that had driven me away from Kit, and then brought me right back here to where I belonged.

Other animals might have been startled by my actions. Other creatures might have run from the force of the sound, but those wolves–those wise, beautiful creatures–they didn't flinch. They sat there, still as stone and just as solid. They were patient and understanding souls and they understood tears.

When the sobs were almost gone, Andak sat up. He nuzzled my face and then lay down beside me. I let my hand drop over the side of the chair to tangle my fingers in the scruff of his neck. I was so very tired and I was beginning to get more frightened. Why was Kit not back yet? He said latest three days. In fact, he seemed sure he'd be back after two days.

I closed my eyes and prayed. "Please sweet Jesus. Don't take him away from me too. Not now. Not like this. I won't be able to survive this."

Even as the whisper died on my lips I heard the sound of a car. It was not the same car that came the other night, but it was a car, and it was turning into the road. I stood up. The wolves were already up and scattering away. I walked to the porch and began to go down the steps. Andak was shadowing me. The car stopped halfway down the drive and I began to walk down the road. Why did they stop there? Was something wrong?

“Kit,” I screamed, taking another step. It was a careless step and suddenly I was pitched forward. To my surprise an even greater force than what propelled me forward hit me just above my heart and sent me flying backwards.

The pain was like a flash. White hot pain embedded itself into my flesh. I landed on the ground on my back, my head banging the hard ground with a loud thud, but I did not feel a thing. My hand reached to the burning wound under my shoulder blade.

Something long and hard was buried deep in me.

The car drove up. Everything was happening in slow motion. I groaned in pain. The car stopped. The door opened. Snow crunched under someone’s boot. Even though I was terrified my brain was razor sharp.

“Sawyer?” I called.

Someone stood a few feet away from me. “I’m sorry, Lara. I’m really sorry. I didn’t mean to hit you. You fell. I was aiming for the wolf.”

“It’s okay, Sawyer.” My voice was trembling. “I know you didn’t mean to shoot me. It was just an accident.”

“I’m really sorry, Lara. I love you.”

“I know. Just help me. Take me to the hospital.”

There was a strangled sound, then Sawyer began to cry. “I can’t help you, Lara. No one can know I was here.”

"Please, Sawyer. I won't tell anyone."

"You're lying. Of course, you'll tell them."

"They'll know by your arrow, anyway."

"I'm going to pull it out of you."

"Please, Sawyer. Don't do this. I'll die out here."

"You shouldn't have been here. Why did you come here?"

"Sawyer, shooting me was an accident. If you pull the arrow head out and leave me here to die it will be murder."

"Shut up," he screamed.

"You won't get away with it."

"I can't leave my arrow here," he snarled, and took a step towards me and suddenly there was the sound of a low growl, more menacing than I ever could have imagined. So deep and guttural it was almost otherworldly. I heard the other wolves start moving in from all sides.

With a scream of terror Sawyer ran back to his car. I heard his door slam shut, and he reversed out of the driveway like a madman, his tires spinning in the snow and ice.

The pain started radiating outwards. The house was a few feet away. If I could just make it back. I tried to sit up, but I couldn't move at all.

Then I heard a bloodcurdling growl close to me. Lobo! I could sense it was him, but he was different. This was not the wolf that climbed on top of me and playfully licked me. I suddenly remembered the freak cases of owners of big dangerous dogs being attacked and killed by their pets when they had suffered a heart attack or seizures, and fallen to the ground. I was no longer a friend. I was prey. I began to shake. I heard the other wolves moving in. Lobo was not protecting me. He was warning the other wolves off his kill. It was the pecking order.

They were going to eat me!

I opened my mouth to scream and frighten them off when I felt powerful jaws close in on my good shoulder. Pure fear took over. Kit's wolves were going to eat me alive.

The fear was such that I blacked out.

Forty-five

Kit

https://www.youtube.com/watch?v=QNXL_-oLJU8

I saw the faint orange glow in the windows from the top of the driveway and every cell in my body solidified with horror. What the fuck? She was in my house while I was not there! While that dangerous stalker was still running around?

"The lights are on in your place, man," Billy said.

The road was pure ice and I could run faster than the car could drive up. "Stop the car," I shouted as I pulled the handle, and jumping onto thick snow ran as quickly as I could to the house. The wolves were on the porch, gathered around something. My heart was pounding like crazy.

In one horrified glance I saw the marks in the snow my wolves had made when they dragged whatever they were guarding along the driveway and up the steps onto the porch.

I put my boot on the first step and even before I saw her, I saw the arrow. My wolves did not come to me, lick my hands, or show their usual greetings. They stood up and slunk away nervously to the edges of the porch.

I dropped in front of her. The warmth of the animals had permeated the whole area, creating a little oasis of heat in the dead of winter. She looked pale, but just the way she did when she was asleep. I touched her neck. Her skin was cold, and her pulse weak, but she was still alive. I touched the area around the arrow. She made no sound.

I shook the shaft very gently and I knew that it was not lodged in bone. Fortunately, the arrow had missed her scapula. An arrow that powerful would have shattered her scapula like a commemorative Elvis plate and damaged it forever, but it was unlikely that she had been lucky enough that it passed through the only safe place it could in that area, a triangle smaller than the size of her open mouth.

Even if there weren't any serious internal injuries, the arrow head would have to be located and removed. I yanked the arrow out of Chepi's dead body, but I couldn't pull it out of Lara. It would have ripped the head off and left it in her body.

A smooth bullet could be safely allowed to remain encased in bone or tissue, but an arrow head was sharp and rough, and would continue to injure and inflame the tissue around it, ultimately resulting in infection and death.

The local hospital had closed its doors three years earlier, and the nearest one was nearly an hour away. In these road conditions it was an hour and a half journey at least, but there were no other options.

I could hear Billy running up the driveway. Carefully, I lifted her up in my arms, and hoisted her up.

"What the fuck happened?" he said behind me.

"We need to take her to the doctor." My voice was shockingly calm.

We got her into the car and I wrapped her in my coat and held her close to me. She moaned a few times, but I spoke softly to her and she drifted off to sleep. I was afraid. I was very afraid of what was happening inside her body. That hour and half turned out to be the longest hour and half of my life. I thought it would never end. I felt so helpless I wanted to smash something or scream.

As soon as we arrived at the emergency doors, my buddies had to disappear. They couldn't even be seen in that location. I carried her in and yelled for help. They were quick to respond and she was wheeled away from me. I went to the waiting room and stood gazing blankly out of the window. A small girl was waiting with her mother. She skipped up to me. I could see her reflection in the glass. She was blonde with pigtails. Her dress was pink with little blue and white boats on the front.

"Are you here to repair your face?" she asked me.

"Holly, come here and stop bothering everyone," her mother scolded.

She skipped away.

I looked at my hands. They were full of dried blood. I could cry for Chepi and Roger, but I couldn't cry for Lara. The pain was too great. The thought of losing her was incomprehensible, intolerable. The thought that I had left her in danger made me so angry I wanted to hurt myself by punching the walls.

I went to a chair and sat down. The little girl was playing with blocks. She didn't approach me again. Someone came to call the mother and they left the room. I was alone. I didn't move. I just sat there as if I was stoned until the doctor came. He was an overweight, middle-aged, balding man. He wore steel-rimmed glasses. Behind them his eyes were a watery blue.

"Mr. Carson?"

"Yes," I replied standing up. My legs felt like jelly; they felt as if they could barely hold me upright.

He smiled. "She's going to be all right."

That was when tears filled my eyes. Tears of pure happiness. "Can I see her?" I asked.

"You can, but she's still unconscious."

"Thank you," I whispered. It was one of those moments. If he had asked me to get on my knees and suck his dick, I would have. I felt so grateful, I wanted to kiss him.

"She's one lucky girl. The arrow broke her third rib and passed right through, nicking her lung, and causing it to fill up with blood. We sorted that out. It also broke her fourth rib on the left side on its way out."

"I thought you said she was lucky," I croaked. I had prayed her lungs would not be touched.

"The arrowhead was millimeters away from scraping her brachial artery. If it had it would have been like pulling the drain on a bathtub. She would have bled out into her body cavity and been dead in minutes.

My heart felt as if it was on fire. To think she had come that close! Silently, I followed the doctor into the little room she was in. She looked small, white, and pitiful. There were bleeping machines all around her.

A nurse came in and I asked if I could sit and wait for her to wake up, because I wanted the first thing she felt when she woke up to be my hand.

She smiled kindly. "I don't see why not."

That was what Lara felt when she came around a few hours later: Me sitting up on a chair holding her hand.

"Kit," she mumbled.

"I'm here. I'm never leaving you again."

"My heart and chest hurts," she whispered.

"I know, baby. I know. I'm sorry."

"What happened to me?"

"Shh ... Rest now. We'll talk about it later."

I stood up and kissed her forehead, and waited for her to drift back to sleep. I watched the even movement of her chest, then I walked out of her room. It was already light outside.

In the car park I found my pickup. As we had agreed, the guys drove my pickup here and left the key behind the visor. I got into it and drove into town where I found a diner and went in for breakfast.

I ordered a big breakfast, the whole works, and I ate it like a starving man. I drank two cups of black coffee, then I went to the phone box at the side of the restaurant and called Sheriff

Bradley. I told him what had happened and asked him if he could tell Elaine about the incident.

"Was there any evidence left behind?" Sheriff Bradley asked.

"Nope. None at all. You don't have any clues, do you?"

"Not off the top of my head. Must be kids foolin' around your place again. I'll have to send out a stern warning."

"I'd appreciate that, Sheriff. Mighty good of you to do that. I'll be right here in Tapley for the next few days," I said. "I saw a motel as I was passing, I'll probably check in there."

"What's it called?"

"The Big Blue."

"Yeah, I know it. If anything comes up, I'll let you know."

"Much appreciated, Sheriff. Much appreciated."

Forty-six

Kit

As I expected, Elaine came rushing through the doors before lunch. She looked white-faced and frightened. I was waiting at reception waiting and as soon as I heard her say Lara's name I walked up to her.

"Elaine?" I asked.

She whirled around. Pretty girl, auburn hair, big, green eyes, and one of those cupid mouths that was no longer popular, but I thought was rare and special. She was taller and curvier than Lara. She was exactly Roger's type. If he'd been here he'd have gone for her big time.

"Kit Carson," she gasped, clutching her chest as if I was Count Dracula himself.

I stretched my lips into the most friendly shape I could twist them into. "Yup, that's me."

"Ah, right. How is Lara?"

"She'll be all right."

She sagged with relief.

"She's sleeping right now. Come on. I'll take you to her."

The lift was ancient and very slow. We didn't speak. Once her eyes slid sideways, and then dropped away very quickly when she met my eyes. She cleared her throat and looked up at the lighted numbers above her head. When the door creaked open, slower than an old coffin, I indicated the way.

I opened the door and saw that Lara was still asleep. Elaine moved quickly towards the bed. Normally, I would have waited outside and given her some privacy, but I was curious to see her reaction.

She looked down at Lara and began to sob softly. That told me everything I needed to know. I knew then I could trust Lara with her. Quietly, I slipped out of the room. I leaned against the wall and waited for her to come out.

When the door opened, I straightened. “Can I buy you a coffee from the vending machine?”

“Yeah,” she said and smiled weakly.

We walked to the machine. “Want a candy bar?”

She shook her head. I dropped some coins into the slot and got us our coffees. They were truly terrible, but I needed an excuse and I could drink a million cups of coffee if it was going to help Lara. I guided her towards a nest of sofas.

“I can’t understand it. Sheriff Bradley said there had been a hunting accident. I dropped her off at your place. She was just fine when I left at about 7:00 p.m. What happened?” she asked, sniffing and wiping her nose with a tissue.

“When I came back, I found her with an arrow buried in her body.”

Her eyes narrowed and glinted with suspicion. This was no naïve girl. She was bristling with intelligence. “An arrow?”

"Why do you think Sheriff Bradley told you it was a hunting accident when it is not even hunting season?"

"What do you think happened?" she asked cautiously. She had just turned the tables on me.

"I think Lara has a dangerous admirer," I said, watching her closely.

She stared steadily into my eyes. "Sawyer. His name is Sawyer Buchannan."

"Is he engaged to be married to someone else?"

"Yes."

"Is his fiancée from a rich family?"

"The richest." Her voice was hard.

"Why do you think it was him?"

"Because he's always had a thing for her, but he couldn't resist the lure of high cotton, of being Rhett Haverbrooke's son-in-law."

I nodded.

"Are you going to talk to him?"

"No, I'll leave him to Sheriff Bradley. Can't take the law into my own hands."

For a second she frowned. Then she smiled. A big sunny grin. "Yes, I think that is the best way forward. I like that idea. That way everybody gets exactly what they deserve."

"Everybody gets what they deserve," I repeated softly.

"What are the doctors saying about Lara? When can she go home?"

"Barring no complications I'll probably be able to take her back in a week, but her recovery will take about six to eight weeks. She'll have to take it easy during that time."

"That's good. I guess I better go see if she's awake."

"That's a fine idea. She'll be happy to see you."

She nodded and walked away. I watched her throw away her untouched coffee cup into a bin, but my mind was already busy thinking of something else.

I'd say this for Sawyer Buchannan. He had the decency to make it super easy for me to hunt him down. He drank at the local watering hole.

I watched him come out of the bar swaying drunk and get into his car. Then I followed him until he got onto a quiet stretch of road. When he was nearly upon an area where the trees thinned out on one side of the road, I put on my illegal police siren.

He pulled over instantly. Very compliant.

The shock on his face when he saw, not one of his law enforcement friends, but me appear at his window paid for his birth certificate. I wish I had a picture.

"What do you want?" he blustered drunkenly.

I didn't waste time talking. I punched him by the side of his face and knocked his lights out. Then I started walking back to my pickup. If anyone came by they'd think he was passed out.

I drove my vehicle into the woods and parked it out of sight. Whistling, I walked back to his car and pulled him into the passenger seat. Fortunately for me I never met a single person on the road as I drove him back to my place.

I threw him over my shoulder, carried him into the forest behind my house, and dumped him in the hole I had dug earlier. To my surprise he woke up and looked around him blearily.

"What are you doing?" he demanded. He sounded belligerent and frightened.

"It's good that you woke up for your funeral," I said coldly.

He tried to stand up. I took my gun and shot his kneecaps out. Two bullets. I'm a crack shot.

Whoa, what a racket. I'd seen a lot of men die in my time, but he took the cake. I stared at him curiously. I'd never enjoyed killing before, but watching him suffer actually made digging the hole worth it. Winter ground is a bitch to open and I broke my back doing it.

While he was still screaming with pain and horror, I picked up my shovel, and began to chuck cold dirt on him. You should have seen the way he clawed to get out. Every time he put his hands at the edge of the hole I smacked them with the shovel.

It was torture pure and simple.

He lay in his grave and tried to explain. Something about it being an accident. That fell on deaf ears. He started apologizing. Should have said his last rites instead. He begged, he cried, he threatened, he promised, he shouted, he cursed, but nothing stopped the earth from falling. Eventually, his mouth was filled with earth and even the muffled choking and gasping sounds were gone.

Silence was restored to my land.

Swinging my shovel, I returned to my house. I removed the plates from his fancy car and put new ones on. Ten minutes later my buddy Grayson and his pal Ted came by. Ted drove off in the car they had come in, and Grayson and I got into Sawyer's car and drove to the spot where my pickup was hidden. He said goodbye and I got into my pickup. We went our separate ways.

No money changed hands.

Forty-seven

Lara

A week went by in the hospital. Kit and I never talked about that day. I knew he didn't want to stress me and it suited me fine because I knew I wanted to wait until I was at his home before I told him my decision. Today was my last day at the hospital and Kit had gone to get some medication when a man came in.

"Hello, Lara," he greeted. His voice was cultured, but steely. "You don't know me, but I'm Rhett. Rhett Haverbrooke."

I drew my breath in so sharply it hurt my lung. I relaxed my body and took a few shallow breaths.

"I'm sorry if I startled you," he said, coming closer.

"What do you want?" I asked suspiciously. I didn't want any trouble with Mr. Haverbrooke's powerful family.

"I wanted to thank you."

My body stilled with astonishment. "Thank me? For what?"

"For taking care of my problem."

I frowned. "Problem? What problem?"

"My daughter was about to marry a worthless gold-digger. Nothing I could say would make her change her mind. Sheriff Bradley tells me thanks to you, young lady, he seems to have completely disappeared from the scene. Run away with his tail between his legs."

"Oh, that," I said softly. "Yes, it is a good thing Kayleigh did not marry him. He was not a good man."

"Well," he breathed out. "I thought I'd drop by and let you know that I'd like to return the favor. If ever you are in need of something, don't hesitate to call on me. If you need anything at all. Money? Whatever? Just contact me."

I shook my head. "Thank you kindly, but I don't need anything, Mr. Haverbrooke." Then I stopped. "Actually, I do need something. Do you have connections in Hollywood?"

"I believe I do," Mr. Haverbrooke said, and I could hear the smile on his face.

"Good, because I've got a friend that could do with a bit of help. You mustn't tell her though. It has to be done in secret."

"Well then, it'll be our little secret," he said as Kit came into the room.

"You must be Kit. I'm Rhett," he said civilly.

"Pleased to meet you," Kit said, but his voice was cold and hard.

"The pleasure is all mine. You and Lara should come around for dinner. Meet my wife and daughter."

"I'm not one for going out much, Rhett, but thank you kindly for the offer."

"Well, I'll be going then. Good day to both of you."

"I'll contact you about my friend. Her name is Elaine."

"What was that about?" Kit asked me.

I gleefully told him about Rhett Haverbrooke's offer to help.

A nurse pushed me out of the hospital in a wheelchair, and Kit helped me into the pickup.

"Are you all right?" he asked.

"Yes."

"Remember, if at any time you feel shortness of breath, sudden sharp chest pain, fever over 101° or the incision starts weeping, tell me immediately because we have to go back to the hospital," he said worriedly.

I nodded. "Okay."

"Okay. You ready to go home?"

"Yeah." I smiled at him.

It felt strange after a week of the sterile air of the hospital to breathe in fresh, cold air again. It hurt my lung a bit, but I enjoyed the feeling of bitter cold air going into my system again, even if it did sting my lung some.

We didn't talk much in the car. I was tired, but happy. Very happy. I might even have dozed off. When I woke up again Kit was parking the car. His skin touched mine–so warm, as if he had just removed a pair of fleece-lined gloves. He squeezed my good shoulder, then bent to kiss my forehead.

"Are you okay?" he asked, and there was a softness that spoke volumes.

"Yeah," I said slowly.

"Let's go inside," he said softly.

Kit came around to my side, and gently, as if I was made from spun sugar, helped me down. "Shall I carry you to the door?" he asked.

"What, and have you drop me in the snow?" I joked.

He didn't laugh. Slowly, step by step, he led me to the door. He opened it and I heard the unmistakable clicking of a wolf's claws on the hardwood floor behind me. I gasped in amazement. I hadn't heard him come up. "Is it Lobo?" Kit told me how he found me surrounded by wolves.

When I told him that Lobo had growled at me, he said that Lobo was growling to the others. Warning them to keep away from his human. He explained that when Lobo took my shoulder in his jaw he had done it to drag me along the driveway. Somehow, he managed to pull me up the steps to the porch. Then the wolves had sat around me guarding and keeping me warm.

"Yes," Kit said, his voice kinder than I had ever heard.

I smiled for the first time in a long while. "He wants to come with me. He's my buddy."

"If you want in, boy, you go right ahead," Kit said.

"I thought the wolves were not really allowed into the house."

Kit tightened his arm around me and dropped a kiss onto my hair. "He saved your life, Lara. As far as I'm concerned, he can have my bed."

I bit my lip. “I feel bad that I even for a moment thought they were going to eat me when I owe my life to Lobo and the rest of them.”

“Hey, don’t worry about it. They don’t know and even if they did, animals don’t keep grudges. You were frightened and you were right to be cautious.”

“I’m glad they’ll never know,” I said softly.

“I’ll be damned. It looks like he’s going to curl up in front of the fire just like a dog.”

“I guess that’s where I will curl up, too,” I said, and walked to towards the hearth.

A few minutes later we were all huddled around the fireplace as Kit made the fire roar. Lobo pressed against my feet, the warmth of his big body instantly cut through the chill. I reached down to scratch his ears.

“We need to talk,” Kit said.

“I agree. You go first.”

“Look ... I know I lied, and that was wrong. Very wrong. I’m very sorry about that.” Kit stood up and began to pace the floor. “I know when we parted the last time you said you never wanted to see me again, but I want to say something first, and then you can decide if you still want us to break up.”

I opened my mouth to tell him I would have him even if it was only for a day, but Kit cut me off. “Please, just listen to me first.”

“Okay,” I agreed quietly.

Forty-eight

Lara

https://www.youtube.com/watch?v=m5N9IHqqGcA

"I know I went away without any explanation of where I was going, or what I would be doing, but you have to understand that there are some things I just can't tell you. That I will never be able to talk about. I will have to keep those secrets to myself, simply because ... I took an oath.

"All I can tell you is that I was sent to another country. It was a dangerous job. We were dealing with people who would have cut your hand off for your watch. I wish I could tell you everything, but all I can say is that it was a partial success. We didn't get the bad guys but we got the guns and the drugs.

He paused.

"Anyway, there was a lot of gunfire going on and confusion, and my best buddy... Roger, I never told you about him because he was always a part of my other life. I didn't know how to tell you about him without telling you everything else as well, but I can tell you about him now, I think.

"Roger and I went into the service together. He was a Ranger for a long time before he switched over to the dark side, as he liked to say.

He worked with me in special ops. He was as badass as they come. We went through everything together. He was there for me. Every mission, he was there.

"Roger was a beer connoisseur. He laid his motorcycle down once because a car braked too fast in front of him, and he swore that was the only time he actually saw his life flash before his eyes. After that he was butch enough to lead a crew into hellfire, but he was too pussy to get on a motorcycle again."

Kit sat and sighed.

"He had these magnetic brown eyes. The man was a fucking monster. We used to go on these trips to exotic beaches where he always got laid, sometimes three or four times in a night, and the most I got was sand in all the wrong places. He ... he was brave and strong but he cried like a little boy when his dog died ..."

Kit took a deep breath.

"He's gone, Lara. He died in my arms on this last trip. He was standing in the wrong place at the wrong time and we didn't see it coming until it was too late."

Kit's voice was raw with hurt and sadness and it damn near broke my heart to hear him in that way. There was nothing I could do. His best friend would never return. I reached out to touch his shoulder. I felt Lobo push closer to him, and Kit wrapped an arm around the big wolf. He laid his head on my knee.

"He's gone, and I'm not going back, Lara. I'm out."

"You're what?" My mind was reeling, thoughts bouncing back and forth like I was in a pinball machine. "What does that mean?"

"It means exactly what you think it means," he said.

My heart leaped with disbelief.

"I'm done with the military," he confirmed. "I only have a few more months before I have to make the decision on whether to re-enlist. I'm not going to do it. I was going to ... this job has been my life. But I've realized that I can't have a life with someone if I stay with this."

I swallowed hard. I wanted so much for what he was saying to be real, but I dare not. "Kit, sometimes people make rash decisions when they are grieving ..."

"I know that, but this isn't a knee-jerk reaction. Roger and I promised each other we would retire together. He didn't get to retire the way he wanted, but he insisted that I should ... and I agree. I'm done, honey. For real. For good.

"And I know that it might not matter to you at this point. I know that you probably still plan to tell me goodbye. And that's okay. I did lie to you. I kept things from you. I can understand if you want to go, but I have to warn you I won't, I can't let you go. Ever. You're mine.

"You were mine from the day you walked out of that blue Toyota. You were as clean and as wholesome as an apple. I took one look at you and thought, she's blind, but she's shining with light and I can see, but I'm living with darkness. I survived because of you. You're the reason I wake up in the morning, Lara. I ain't going to stop asking you to marry me. I've good knees so I can stay on bended knee for as long as it takes."

"Kit." I squeezed his shoulder and pulled him closer to me. "Now it's my turn to talk. Okay?"

I took several deep breaths, trying to center myself, hoping that I wouldn't cry. Stupid idea, as tears were already welling up and spilling onto my cheeks. "I came to your house that night because I had already made my decision. It was Elaine that made me realize that even if it was only one day I could have with you, I'd rather have that than nothing. No matter what suffering I have to go through you are worth every second of any kind of pain."

Kit's hand tightened on mine.

"It's only when you went away that I really realized just how much I love you. I knew I loved you, but I never understood how deeply. I love you so much I felt like dying without you. I couldn't eat. I couldn't sleep. I couldn't even function normally. I just sat at home in my pajamas until Elaine came around and then I quickly changed into some clothes and tried to pretend that I was normal."

"Wait ... what did you say?"

I smiled through the tears. "Very funny."

When Kit turned and threw his arms around me, Lobo had enough. He wiggled and got out of the way with a sound that was almost a sigh, as though he was a human who was tired of this nonsense. I listened as he curled up by the front door, and I imagined he was looking back at us with the air of a teenager dealing with mom and dad showing too much affection in his presence.

I pulled away from Kit. “Kit, Mr. Haverbrooke said that Sawyer just upped sticks and left town after he shot me, but that can’t be true. I mean, I know he was a coward, but he would have figured he could fix anything once he’d married Kayleigh. Sawyer hasn’t left town, has he?”

“I only ever lied the once to you, Lara. I won’t do it again. You sure you want to know the truth?”

“I do. We’re in this together. No matter. If you go down, I go down.”

“I let it go when he killed Chepi, but he crossed the line when he left you for dead. A psychopath won’t stop, and as long as he walked this earth I knew no one I loved would be safe. I couldn’t trust the Sheriff to do the right thing. So I took care of it myself.”

“He’s dead?” I asked.

“He’s gone, Lara. He’s never coming back. All that matters to me is you and my wolves are safe and this land is at peace.” Kit’s voice changed. “As long as I live no one will ever hurt you again my Princess.”

In my heart I knew that Kit was right. Sawyer was criminally insane, and God only knew what he might have eventually done to Kayleigh. What if he’d kept his threat to come back for me? I sent a silent prayer of gratitude that could never happen now.

“What happens if anybody finds out?” I asked.

"I took steps to ensure that won't ever happen. The earth will keep my secret long after we are gone."

Kit pulled me to him and held me so tightly it was hard to breathe. I finally had to push on his chest with both hands, just a little, to give us both enough space. I wasn't done with what I had to say.

"Sorry," he apologized immediately.

"So I decided that I would take you as you are, and learn to deal with the fact that you were in the military. Now that you tell me you are leaving it, I am ecstatically happy not to have to be left alone for days not knowing if you are alive or dead. But either way, I'm here, and I'm not leaving."

"Say that again," he said, his words highlighted by his teasing tone.

"That I'm not leaving?"

"No. The other thing."

"I sure do love you, you sexy hunk."

Kit laughed as he pulled me close again, crushing me against his chest. "I love you too, you sassy, sweet, beautiful pain in my butt. You don't know what I went through when I saw you lying on the porch. Fuck, I couldn't go through that again. I thought for sure it was goodbye ..."

"Kit," I whispered against his jaw.

"Yeah?"

"Now shut up and show me how much you love me."

He laughed against my lips before he stood up, slipped his arms underneath me, and lifted me as though I weighed nothing at all. His strong steps took us towards the stairs. “We don’t want Lobo to see this. I don’t want him getting ideas. You’re mine and he has to go find his own girl,” he said.

He lowered me to the bed and his hands immediately went to my blouse. “Let me show you just how much I fucking love you,” he said, opening my blouse one button at a time, kissing the exposed skin as he made his way down.

“Go on then,” I whispered, and he did. Over and over.

Forty-nine

Kit

https://www.youtube.com/watch?v=vGJTaP6anOU

"Do you want to come in with me or wait here?" I asked Lara.

"I'll wait here. You go and do what you have to," she said, and smiled at me.

"Okay, I won't be long." I kissed her and jumped out of the truck. I walked up to the front door of a small house with an immaculate lawn. A woman opened the door.

"Hey, Marla," I greeted.

Her mouth dropped open. "Kit. What are you doing here?"

"I was passing through and just thought I would stop by. Where's Mike?"

"At work," she said slowly.

"Kids at school?"

"Yeah. You want to come in?" The years had not been so kind to her. There was something sad about her.

"Sure," I said.

"You got someone in the car?"

"That's my girl Lara."

"Doesn't she want to come in?"

"No, she's got a Dolly Parton CD on. Country music hurts my ears, so she has to find opportunities to listen when I'm not around." I smiled at her.

With an answering smile she opened the door wider, and I stepped into a neat space. There were floral curtains at the windows all tied up with pretty ribbons, and the sofas looked like miniature versions of the real thing. It was a bit like being in a doll's house.

She waved her hand towards the largest sofa. "Can I get you something to drink?"

"Thanks, but I'm all right," I said.

She nodded and went to perch on a pink armchair opposite. Clearing my throat uncomfortably, I folded my giant form into the little sofa.

"So ... what did you want to tell me?"

"I wanted to tell you about Roger."

She frowned. "Roger? What about him?"

"He's gone. He passed on."

Her hands rushed to clasp her face. "No," she whispered.

"I'm sorry, Marla."

She looked confused. "How?"

"Would you believe me if I told you someone pulled a gun on him in the car park of a bar. He got shot in the neck and died. No one knows who did it."

She shook her head. "No, I'd have to call you a liar. Nobody could pull a gun on Roger in the parking lot of a bar. He was too fast."

"That's the official version."

She stared at me, her eyes wide. "Why does Roger's death need an official version?"

"Why do you think?"

Her face paled and her hands clenched. "I thought he left the army."

I looked at her and said nothing.

She breathed out. "Oh my God. It all makes sense now."

"I'm so sorry, Marla."

She nodded a few times. A phone rang somewhere in the house and she jumped up. "I have to answer that," she said distractedly.

"Sure, go ahead."

I heard her pick up the call in the hallway. "Oh, good," she said. "That'll be great. Yeah. No, no, everything is fine. I'm fine. I was dusting the house. Some dust in my throat. It's fine. Everything is just fine. I'll see you tonight. What? Oh, uh. Meatloaf. Yeah. Whatever you want. Yeah. I can make that too. Sure. Sure. No. I think there's another carton of cookie dough ice cream in the freezer. Right. I'll see you when you get home."

For a few minutes there is no sound at all then I hear her footsteps come back to the living room.

"That was Mike," she said.

I smiled politely.

"I love Mike."

I didn't know what to say. I nodded. "I know."

"He's a good man. He stood by me. I can trust him. You should leave now."

"Roger had a message for you."

Her mouth dropped open. “A message? For me?”

“Yeah, he died in my arms. You were the last thing on his mind.”

Her legs just gave way and she collapsed to the floor. I rushed to help her to the sofa. “Shall I get you a glass of water?”

“No, get me that bottle of whiskey over there.”

I walked up to the little tray, picked up the bottle of whiskey, and turned to her. “Where are the glasses?”

“Just bring the bottle,” she said harshly.

I gave her the bottle and she swigged from it like a sailor. She must have drunk a quarter of the bottle’s contents. Then she closed her eyes. When she opened them they were different. “What’s the message?”

“He wanted you to know he loved you. There was no one else for him. Ever.”

She blinked very quickly. “Then why did he leave me?”

“He wanted to protect you. He knew he would leave you a widow. He didn’t want that for you.”

She began to cry then. Softly then harder and harder. “That was not his decision to make. I’ve lost everything. He broke my heart, Kit. He broke my heart.”

“It was the job, Marla. It broke us all.”

“You know what he used to say?”

“What?”

“He used to say there would be no more wars if politicians had to send their sons to fight.”

"Yeah, and how right he was."

She swallowed and stood up. "Thank you for coming here."

"No problem." I turned to leave. "Look, I can see myself out."

"Kit?"

"Yeah?"

"You remember that time we all went up to the mountain?"

I smiled sadly at the memory. It was the last time we were all together. "Yeah, sure."

"We got married, you know? We exchanged rings under the moonlight and he swore to me that he would never love anybody else."

"He kept his promise, Marla."

"So did I," she whispered, so softly I almost didn't hear.

Fifty

Lara

https://www.youtube.com/watch?v=jorJh8DTMVM

"Who all is out there, then?" I asked.

Elaine walked to the door and opening it a crack, peeked out into the church interior. We were in the small room built to the side of the Church. It was really a sort of storeroom, but the minister had allowed us to use it for this occasion.

"Well?' I prompted nervously.

Elaine shut the door and came back to stand in front of me. Her voice trembled slightly. "Are you sure you want to know?"

"You mean no one came?" I whispered shocked and sad, even while another part of me rebelled. So what if the townspeople did not turn up for my wedding. I didn't care. They and their high and mighty, self-righteous sensibilities could go to hell. I was getting married today to the man of my dreams. Nothing, and no one, was going to spoil that for me.

Elaine took my hand in both of hers. "No one came? The church is packed to the rafters, Lara."

"What?"

"I've never seen anything like it. Everyone has come to see you get married. Heck even Rhett Haverbooke. He brought his wife and all six of his brats. Snooty cow Kayleigh looks like she's chewing on a handful of hornets, but she's out there in her Sunday best too."

"Really?" I gasped.

"And guess who else is there? Loopy Luther. Sitting in the front row."

"Marybeth Luther came to witness me marrying the heathen?"

"Yup. Clutching her rosary and praying for your salvation, no doubt."

I was suddenly nervous. A host of butterflies were fluttering madly in my stomach. "Did you see Kit?"

"You can't exactly miss him. He's bigger than everybody else."

"What's he doing?"

"He turned around and saw me, so I'd say he's waiting impatiently for you."

I smiled. "How do I look?"

"Like a woman who's marrying a heathen," she chirped.

"Are you thinking the red dress is too much now?"

"No, way. I think it's perfect." She touched the little flowers in my hair. "You look bewitching in it, like some kind of forest siren that lures men onto their bloody deaths."

"Elaine?"

"Just kidding. You are the most radiant bride I've ever set eyes on. Hell, I'd marry you myself of Kit wasn't so big and fierce."

I giggled. "You're mad."

"Are you ready?"

I nod.

"Shall I go get my father?"

"Yeah."

She went out and I stood in the stillness of the room alone. I took a deep, calming breath and the strangest thing happened. *I thought my Ma was in the room with me.* The sensation was so strong, I called out. "Ma."

There was no reply, but something that felt like a feather landed on my shoulder.

I didn't move a muscle.

"Ma," I called again. Again, the feather light touch on my hand this time, and suddenly, I understood. My mother had reached out from heaven to bless me on my wedding day. Tears of awe and love filled my eyes, and ran down my face.

"I love you, Ma," I whispered.

Then the door burst open and Elaine came in with her father.

"My goodness me," she exclaimed. "Don't you dare start crying. You're ruining all my good work."

"Stop bullying the poor child," her father scolded. "She can cry on her own wedding day if she wants to."

"Pa, how many times does Ma have to tell you? Stay out of women's business," she said, and began to dab at my face.

I grasped her hand. "My ma was here, Elaine. I felt her."

She became still. “Oh, Lara. What a beautiful thing to happen on your wedding day?”

“It was. It was the most peaceful and beautiful thing that has ever happened to me.”

“What did it feel like?”

“It was just a feather light touch and the sensation that she was in the room with me.” I paused. “She was happy for me, Elaine. Very happy.” More tears flowed from my eyes.

“I’m so glad for you, Lara, but now, you’ve got to stop the waterworks, or all my hard graft will be for nothing.”

I was still trembling while she repaired what I had ruined. Then, she thrust my bouquet into my hand and guided me towards her dad’s arm. I laid my hand on it, and he led me out into the church where my beautiful future waited with open arms.

Epilogue

Kit

Three months later

The waves roared, one after the other, constant motion that created the most soothing sound I had ever heard. I dug my toes into the sand and watched as a pretty woman in a bikini walked by. Then I looked again to my right, to the incomparably beautiful woman in a sleek one-piece suit, her hair cascading down her shoulders, her eyes closed, her toes pushed into the sand, and her head tilted back to catch the sun's rays and the soft breezes.

As we listened to the waves roll in, I described the scene around us: the ladies in their bikinis, the colorful towels spread on the sand, the surfers trying to catch a wave and doing a shit job of it. It was not weather for surfing. I told her about the kids and the sandcastles they were building down the beach. I told her the sky was so blue it looked almost unreal, so clear that if I stared at it too long, I would get dizzy.

Condensation ran down the ice bucket in little rivulets of cold. I ran my fingers through it and then touched Lara's thigh. She jumped and laughed at me. "Stop being so evil."

I leaned in and kissed her. "Wanna beer?"

"Yeah," she said.

I opened it up with a delicious hiss and handed the ice-cold bottle to her. I opened up my own and looked over at her. She raised her beer in the air and tilted it toward me.

Her wedding band flashed in the light. "To Roger," she said.

"To Roger."

"I wish I had met him."

"He would have loved you. Maybe too much. I might have got jealous."

I watched as she took one long pull of the beer. Then she casually handed her almost-full bottle to me. "That was delicious."

I was puzzled. "Just one sip?"

Lara smiled and leaned back on her chair. "As soon as I have this baby, you can bring me an ice-cold beer at the maternity ward, and I promise I'll drink the whole thing."

I sat straight up, my heart pounding. "*What did you just say?*"

"You heard me," she said smugly.

I stared at my wife. She leaned her head back and smiled up at the sun. The news hit me in the gut and gave me the strangest feeling, a warmth that was entirely different from anything else I had ever experienced. I reached over to take her hand. "You're sure?"

She nodded and pulled my hand up to kiss my fingers. "And I was thinking ... if it's a boy, we can name him Roger."

Tears stung my eyes. This woman had brought everything I ever dreamed of into my life, and now she was giving me even more. I looked at her flat belly, thinking about how wonderful it would be to see it grow.

"I love you," I said against her hand.

"I love you too," she replied, and we sat together in our little cocoon of happiness, with our little secret deep in her belly, and somewhere, my old friend Roger was laughing, and sipping a beer in our honor.

Lara

Six months later

https://www.youtube.com/watch?v=Id_UYLPSn6U

"Hey. How's it going in Cloneland?" I asked as soon as I heard Elaine's voice on the phone.

Cloneland was Elaine's nickname for Hollywood. When she first arrived there she was stunned by how uniformly beautiful, blonde and tanned all the women were.

"It's shocking how white everyone's teeth are," she whispered the first time she called back. She claimed their teeth were so blinding she had to buy her first pair of sunglasses.

For the last two months she had been, her words, not mine, working her ass off twelve hours a day, six days a week, doing whatever anyone asked her to do for a production designer friend of Haverbrooke, but she was happy. So happy, in fact, she forgot to ask for the latest gossip, not that I'd know any.

"You're not going to believe what just happened to me," she squealed excitedly.

I sat down. "What?" I asked, smiling.

"I think I just sold my screenplay. Remember that production designer friend I told you about?"

"Yeah?"

"Remember how she was going to mention to a producer friend of hers that I had a script?"

"Yeah?"

"The producer asked for the script."

I screamed with joy for her. "So you have to take it to him?"

"It's moved along a bit farther than that."

"What?"

"I didn't want to tell you in case he didn't bother to get back or said he hated it."

"Well."

"He said he loved it that I had a blind heroine, but could I rewrite to make her 13 instead of 17 so she will be more appealing to the tween market."

"Your heroine is blind?"

"Of course."

"What's the story about?"

"It's a story about a blind girl who finds a hurt baby deer in the forest and saves it from the hunters."

"I'm so happy for you, Elaine."

"I owe it all to you. Thank you, Lara."

"Owe it to me? I didn't even know you were writing screenplays."

"You got Haverbrooke to help me, didn't you?"

"No way. I don't even know the man."

"Lara. You are such a lousy liar. I mean, how obvious can you get? I tell you I want to go LA and Haverbrooke's secretary calls me up to offer me a job, and wait for it, in Hollywood, working as what? Oh, yeah, a production director's assistant."

"If your screenplay hadn't been good enough the producer would not have wanted it. You do know that, don't you?"

She laughed. "Yeah, I know that. Okay enough about me. How's the baby coming along?"

"Just fine. We went for the 20 week scan the other day. Kit says she is gorgeous. He says she has my nose."

"That's a good thing. His nose would be too big on a girl."

"Her eyes were closed, but her eyelashes are really long. He said they were so long they were almost an inch long. For the first time in my life I felt sad that I couldn't see."

"Oh, Lara. You will see her soon."

"Yes, I know. I can't wait to feel her little body, her little face, her little hands, hug her, kiss her, smell her. I'm counting the days before I can be her mommy."

"Oh fuck. Someone is calling me. I gotta go, but I'll call you tomorrow."

"Okay, and congratulations, Elaine. I'm real proud of you."

"Thanks," she sang, and making a loud kissing sound, rang off. I lay the phone back on the table and stroked my stomach. I heard the front door open and I began to smile.

Kit's footsteps came across the room towards me. He knelt beside me.

"How are my two girls today?" he asked.

"Missing you," I whispered.

"I got a surprise for you," he said.

I grinned. "What?"

He took my hands and put them in my lap. Then he put something that felt like a plastic or silicone square wrapped in a napkin in my hand. "What is this?" I asked.

"It's your daughter's face."

I frowned. "What? How?"

"It's a 3D printed ultrasound. I sent the ultrasound files to Poland and they produced this."

Speechless, my fingers mapped the little raised face. Her little nose, her lips, her eyes, and then I began to cry with joy.

"Oh, Kit. Thank you. Thank you," I sobbed. "She is so beautiful. Our daughter is a little miracle."

He held me close. "Yes, she is as beautiful as her mother."

"Oh no. She is far more beautiful, and her eyelashes. My goodness. I never thought a baby could have such long lashes."

"I love you, my sweet and wonderful wife," he whispered in my ear.

"I love you too, my wonderful husband, and little baby Carson is the most amazing and splendid treasure I could ever have dreamed of. I'm so glad fate delivered you to Durango Falls, and you went and put up that weird advert at the library."

I felt his breath close to my temple, then he lifted me into his arms.

"Where are you taking me?" I asked, laughing.

"I realized I'd better take advantage of the last few quiet moments we have left before the little one comes."

"What did you have in mind?" I asked as he carried me upstairs.

"I thought I'd put you on your back for a little rest, Mrs. Carson, since you must be very tired, what with being pregnant and all."

Mr. Carson was wrong. Turned out I wasn't tired at all!

THE END

Want To Help An Author?

Please leave a review. Reviews help other readers find an author's work. No matter how short it may be, it is very *precious. Links for your Amazon store below.*

Thank you!

https://www.amazon.com/dp/B01M7YMJK4

https://www.amazon.co.uk/dp/B01M7YMJK4

https://www.amazon.ca/dp/B01M7YMJK4

https://www.amazon.com.au/dp/B01M7YMJK4

Coming Soon...

SUBMITTING TO THE BILLIONAIRE

GEORGIA LE CARRE

One

Nikolai

Thump, thump, thump.

Fucking hell! Someone take my head out of the drum of this washing machine. The wash cycle continues when my cellphone ring vibrates against the bedside table. The sound is like a nail gun going crazy. I unglue my eyes and my lofty, gilded ceiling comes into view.

I'm still in my clothes. I stretch out my arm, fumble around, locate the blasted thing, hold it in front of my face, and squint at it. The screen comes on, blinding me. I hit the green button and put it to my ear.

"Boss, I've been pushing the bell for some time, and didn't get a response. Are you okay?" Semyon's alarmed, booming voice tips the washing machine into spin cycle.

"What time is it?"

"After seven, boss."

"So?"

"At night, boss."

"What?"

I took four pills and decided to lie down for a few minutes, but I must have been more wiped out than I thought. It's Friday and I should have been in the club by seven.

"Bring the car around to the front in fifteen," I instruct, pulling myself off the bed. Rolling my shoulders, I make my way to the bathroom. I open my mirrored cabinet, and take a new box of tablets. Discarding the plastic wrapper, I go into the drawing room and head for the bar. It's an antique, made from wood reclaimed from a Russian church.

Warning. Do not take more than twelve tablets in any twenty-four hour period.

Fuck that. I open the box of tablets and popped out eight pills into the palm of my hand. Grabbing a bottle of Grey Goose, I unscrew the top, and take a generous swig of neat vodka. Nice.

Fortified by the best legal anesthetic available, I go swiftly to the bathroom. In ten minutes, I'm showered and dressed in a fine Saville Row black tailored suit.

I grab my phone and wallet and glance in the hall mirror as I run my fingers through my hair. No time to shave. Still the five o'clock shadow suits how I feel. I set the alarm and open the door, outside the cool Autumn air fills my lungs.

"I've called ahead and spoken with Vanessa Boss. I've informed her you'll be running late and having dinner at 8:30," Semyon says as he opens the rear door of the Maybach.

I nod my approval and slide into the limousine's luxurious interior. Over the smooth purring of the engine, classical music is playing, and the air is scented with expensive perfume. Semyon closes the door for me, and climbs into the front passenger seat. Immediately, Zohar, my driver, sets off to the club. I let my body ease back. Shutting my eyes, I lay my throbbing head on the soft leather headrest.

Were it midweek I sure as hell would not have left the house, but it's Friday. It's the one night I never miss being at the club. It's not the truth, but I tell everybody that it's because Friday night is sucker's night. When the dreamers, the hopers and the scammers, they'll all be along. They go because, of course, life is a complete fantasy-fucking-land.

In their tiny bird brains they think they're just gonna stroll into my club, take the $10,000 Free Stake (which I should say, is like fresh bloodied meat to a Great White shark) and a few hours later they'll have the ticket out of their miserable, pathetic lives, and be rich. Sure, the odd one does good, but that's when the big hook comes out to play. It's called the $100,000 Free Stake. Let me tell you. It's irresistible to the gambling instinct. Even the most cautious gambler will forget that he walked through my front door, the man who never loses.

What does the man who never loses want on a Friday night? Even when his head is fucking killing him?

Awww ... look at you. All curious.

Stick around, cupcake, and maybe you'll see me get it.

Two

Nikolai

Roman and Andrei, my most loyal and reliable security team, are already waiting outside the entrance of Zigurat. It's in a discreet location in a nondescript building. There are no cameras or reporters around here, which is exactly the way I like it. We don't advertise. You have to be recommended by another member to enter. All our punters know exactly what's on offer inside ... and the risks ... of non-payment. This way everything is clear from the start.

Roman opens my door and I slide out. Both Roman and Semyon step into place quickly, one on either side of me, and escort me inside. It sounds like too much? Trust me, you can't be too careful in my business. I have more enemies than friends. Come to think of it. I have no friends. They are all enemies in disguise.

Semyon joins the other two at the front door. His eyes are alert. Good. Inside, I walk through reception, Anastasia, who works the front desk, nods and smiles at me. She doesn't expect me to smile back. I don't.

I head upstairs to the first floor. Roman, who is my chief security team leader remains on my heels. He enjoys his job and takes his task of protecting me very seriously, which I am rather pleased about.

"Good evening Mr. Smirnov," Simone, one of the cocktail waitresses, greets me on the landing. Her smile is wide and promises all kinds of things. She is tall and willowy and shockingly beautiful, and quite honestly, catwalk material. She licks her lips. Yeah, she's nice, real nice, but I don't mix business with pleasure. Actually, who am I kidding. I would mix anything with pleasure, but I'm just not interested. She's a dime a dozen.

"How many in the Blue Room?" I ask her.

"Six, Mr. Smirnov."

"And next door?"

"Six as well."

"Excellent."

"Thank you, Mr. Smirnov."

I look at my watch. Eight-thirty on the nail. I head downstairs and make my way to the purple room, where I normally dine, and where, very occasionally, the richest of the punters are invited to dine here too, but never with me.

Vanessa, a sweet girl, greets me. "Good evening, Sir."

I take a seat. With military precision, a glass of Chateau Petrus arrives. I let its opulence slide over my tongue. Yes, this is the life. In five minutes Vanesa brings seared fillet mignon and girolles in truffle sauce. My head has stopped banging and I enjoy the food.

I skip desert, but accept the small, strong expresso she puts in front of me. Standing up, I make my way back upstairs to my offices, with Roman following silently at my heels. I have to pass reception.

A number of punters are milling around waiting to hand their coats into the cloakroom staff. Some stare, some try to make eye contact, others are oblivious, one or two dash over to shake my hand.

I keep moving never looking their way, and Roman ensures there is no contact. Most are hoping that if they lose and their debt to the club is large, knowing me will make their situation somewhat more favorable. They are wrong.

I pass the main gambling room. As I put my foot on the first step of the stairs that lead to my office, my ears tune to a loud frustrated voice. Every sinew in my body tightens. Slowly, I turn around and look towards the commotion.

"Nico," the man in a sharp pin stripe suit calls. Looking directly at me, he attempts to barge past security and come to me.

Andrei, a six foot six, Special Forces soldier, immediately slaps his huge palm on Nigel's chest, effectively stopping him in his tracks. Well, well, who knew today was the day. I walk towards him, my face wiped clean of the joy and excitement surging in my veins. This is it. This is the moment I have been waiting for.

"You got my money?" I ask.

Nigel's facial expression doesn't alter. "I will. By tonight. I promise."

I raise one eyebrow. "By tonight?"

"Yes, yes, by tonight. You have to let me play tonight and I'll be able to pay you back."

"You don't have the money now."

"No,"

I turn towards Roman.

"Wait," Nigel shouts desperately.

I turn back towards him.

"You see, I had a dream. I dreamt that I would win tonight, so I will. I will win it all back. I can feel it in my bones. You'll get it all back, Mr. Smirnov."

"Take him to the cellar," I instruct.

Roman and Andrei eagerly oblige by quickly frog-marching him down the hall down to the cellar. I walk behind, keeping a small distance. Nigel shouts and pleads over his shoulder. My men take him inside the cellar. There is nothing in that room but a badly stained pool table and a couple of chairs. They have already pushed him down on a chair, by the time I go in.

I close the door quietly behind me and stand for a moment looking at him. Every time I see him I am shocked by how unbelievably pathetic he is. I don't speak, and he rushes to fill the dank silence.

"What are you going to do to me?" he asks, the first signs of real anxiety creeping in.

I shrug. "Nothing ... if I get my money?"

I watch him lean forward in the chair and shuffle his feet. "You're going to get your money Mr. Smirnov. I told you, I had a dream. It was so vivid. I was playing in this club and I just couldn't lose. I won a lot of money. Much more than I owe you. You just need to let me play tonight. Please, I won't lose, I swear. You'll see."

Sudden laughter erupts from my body. Roman and Andrei join in. Our laughter reverberates around the carpetless, curtainless room.

I stop laughing suddenly and step closer. I hold my arms outstretched and Roman comes behind me and removes my jacket. It's just drama. Adds nicely to the tension. Actually, I've never done this before. I suppose I could be a gangster. It's not too bad. I roll up the shirt sleeve of my left arm, and then my right arm. Nigel's eyes dart anxiously from me to my men. His hands are trembling.

"I'll pay you back. I'm good for it."

"You actually thought you could come here without my money, and I would let you play again. You must think I'm fool. Do I look like a fool to you?"

"No, not at all. I know you're not a fool. It was a mistake. Fine, I won't play tonight. I'll get the money. I have the money. I will pay it back."

"You have the money."

"Not, not, right now. But, I ... I ... can get it. Just give me one day."

"One day."

"I'll get it by tomorrow."

"That's not the deal, Nigel. The rules are clear. Every member has three months. Run up as big a debt as you want during that time. Then you have to settle in full. Your three months is tonight."

"But I can settle it tonight. If you just let me play. My dream ..."

"This is no dream, Nigel. This is your fucking reality." I take a step closer. "Put him on the table."

Before the sniveling liar can say another word, he is thrown face down on the pool table.

“Hold his right hand out.” Roman takes one and Andrei the other. I walk slowly towards the wall cabinet, find a hammer. My staff have a sick sense of humor, there is blood still on it. I go back and hold the hammer close enough so that he can see the blood on it.

Please, please Mr. Smirnov. I’ll get you the money.” he begs.

I lift the hammer above my head.

“Wait, Wait,” he screams. “You can have my Mercedes. It’s the latest model, worth one hundred and fifty grand. His eyes are wild in his pale face and there is a nervous tick in his jaw. I try not to smile, as I lower the hammer and put it close to his face. How could he fall for this shit?

“You owe two hundred and fifty grand you piece of shit. What else do you have?”

“Take my house. It's worth one point eight million. You can have everything. Anything. Just let me go." he begs.

That’s the thing about gamblers. Even when they’re in danger of taking their last fucking breath they’ll try to con you.

“Is that all you have?”

“I swear Mr. Smirnov that’s everything I own. I only owe you a quarter of a million, but you can have it all.”

I walk across the room with my back to him. For a few moments, I let the silence ride while I turn inwards. Why Nikolai you’ve won. You’ve played the game, you never flinched, or gave up, and you won again. I smile. Yeah, I won. I turn around and walk back to him.

"Well, Nigel, in that case, you are completely fucked. We both know the bank owns everything you have offered me. Break his hands, boys," I snarl."

"No, no," he sobs. "I beg you don't hurt me. Please."

"I don't understand," he wails. "If you know I have nothing why do you keep asking for what I haven't got? What do you really want?"

I grab a fistful of his sweaty hair and raise his head. His eyes search mine, hoping for a glimmer of vulnerability. He sees none. Only icy cold eyes. He knows this is one debt he must pay. I smile coldly.

"I want your wife, Nigel."

Thank you for reading everybody!

Please click on this link to receive news of my latest releases and giveaways.
http://bit.ly/10e9WdE

and remember

I **LOVE** hearing from readers so by all means come and say hello here:
https://www.facebook.com/georgia.lecarre

24502385R00174

Printed in Great Britain
by Amazon